PAUL AND THE PRINTING PRESS

Also by Sara Ware Bassett

<table>
<tr><td>

THE YOUNG ENGINEERS

Carl and the Cotton Gin
Christopher and the
    Clockmakers
Paul and the Printing Press
Steve and the Steam Engine
Ted and the Telephone
Walter and the Wireless

</td><td>

THE STORY OF

The Story of Glass
The Story of Leather
The Story of Silk
The Story of Sugar
The Story of Porcelain
The Story of Lumber
The Story of Wool

</td></tr>
</table>

This edition published 2026
by Living Book Press
Copyright © Living Book Press, 2026

ISBN: 978-1-76153-462-1 (hardcover)
            978-1-76153-470-6 (softcover)

First published in 1920.

This edition is based on the Little, Brown, and Company printing by 1920.

A catalogue record for this book is available from the National Library of Australia

PAUL AND THE PRINTING PRESS

by

SARA WARE BASSETT

PAUL GAZED UP AT THE PRESSES THAT TOWERED HIGH ABOVE HIS HEAD.

Contents

"… Beneath the rule of men entirely great
The pen is mightier than the sword. Behold
The arch-enchanter's wand!—Itself a nothing—
But taking sorcery from the master-hand
To paralyze the Caesars—and to strike
The loud earth breathless!—Take away the sword—
States can be saved without it!"

—BULWER-LYTTON, *Richelieu*

CHAPTER I

PAUL CAMERON HAS AN INSPIRATION

It was the vision of a monthly paper for the Burmingham High School that first turned Paul Cameron's attention toward a printing press.

"Dad, how much does a printing press cost?" he inquired one evening as he sat down to dinner.

"A *what*?"

"A printing press."

Mr. Cameron glanced up quizzically from the roast he was carving.

"Aren't you a trifle ambitious?"

Paul laughed.

"Perhaps I am," he admitted. "But I have often heard you say, 'Nothing venture, nothing have.'"

It was his father's turn to laugh.

"Yet why does your fancy take its flight toward a printing press?"

Eagerly Paul bent forward.

"Why you see, sir," he explained, "ever since I was chosen President of '20 I've wanted my class to be the finest the Burmingham High ever graduated. I want it to leave a record behind it, and do things no other class ever has. There has never been a school paper. They have them in other places. Why shouldn't we?"

Mr. Cameron was all attention now.

"We've plenty of talent," went on Paul with enthusiasm. "Even Mr. Calder, who is at the head of the English department, asserts that. Dick Rogers has had a poem printed in the town paper—"

He saw a twinkle light his father's eye.

"Maybe you'd just call it a verse," the boy smiled apologetically, "but up at school we call it a poem. It was about the war. And Eva Hardy has had an essay published somewhere and got two dollars for it."

"You don't say so!"

"Besides, there is lots of stuff about the football and hockey teams that we want to print—accounts of the games, and notices of the matches to be played. And the girls want to boom their Red Cross work and the fair they are going to have. There'd be plenty of material."

"Enough to fill a good-sized daily, I should think," remarked Mr. Cameron, chuckling.

Paul took the joke good-naturedly.

"How do people run a paper anyhow?" he questioned presently. "Do printing presses cost much? And where do you get them? And do you suppose we fellows could run one if we had it?"

His father leaned back in his chair.

"A fine printing press is a very intricate and expensive piece of property, my son," he replied. "It would take several hundred dollars to equip a plant that would do creditable work. The preparation of copy and the task of getting it out would also take a great deal of time. Considering the work you already have to do, I should not advise you to annex a printer's job to your other duties."

He saw the lad's face cloud.

"The better way to go at such an undertaking," he hastened to add, "would be to have your publication printed by some established press."

"Could we do it that way?"

"Certainly," Mr. Cameron nodded. "There are always firms that are glad to get extra work if paid satisfactorily for it."

There was a pause.

"The pay is just the rub," Paul confessed frankly. "You see we haven't any class treasury to draw on; at least we have one, but there's nothing in it."

The two exchanged a smile.

"But you would plan to take subscriptions," said the elder man. "Surely you are not going to give your literary efforts away free of charge."

"N—o," came slowly from Paul. Then he continued more positively. "Oh, of course we should try to make what we wrote worth selling. We'd make people pay for it. But we couldn't charge much. Most of us have been paying for our Liberty Bonds and haven't a great deal to spare. I know I haven't."

"About what price do you think you could get for a school paper?"

"I don't know. I haven't thought much about it. Perhaps a dollar, or a dollar and a quarter a year. Not more than that."

"And how many members would be likely to take it?"

Paul meditated.

"There are about fifty seniors," he said. "But of course the other three classes would subscribe—at least some of them would. We shouldn't confine the thing simply to the doings of the seniors. We should put in not only general school news but items about the lower classes as well so that the paper would interest everybody. It ought to bring us in quite a little money.

Shouldn't you think we could buy a press and run it for two hundred dollars?"

"Have you considered the price of paper and of ink, son?"

"No; but they can't cost much," was the sanguine response.

"Alas, they not only *can* but *do*," replied his father.

"Then you think we couldn't have a school paper."

"I did not say that."

"Well, you mean we couldn't make it pay."

"I shouldn't go so far as that, either," returned Mr. Cameron kindly. "What I mean is that you could not buy a printing press and operate it with the money you would probably have at hand. Nevertheless there are, as I said before, other ways of getting at the matter. If I were in your place I should look them up before I abandoned the project."

"How?"

"Make sure of your proposition. Find out how many of your schoolmates would pledge themselves to subscribe to a paper if you had one. Then, when you have made a rough estimate of about how much money you would be likely to secure, go and see some printer and put the question up to him. Tell him what you would want and find out exactly what he could do for you. You've always been in a hurry to leave school and take up business. Here is a business proposition right now. Try your hand at it and see how you like it."

Mr. Cameron pushed back his chair, rose, and sauntered into his den; and Paul, familiar with his father's habits, did not follow him, for he knew that from now until late into the evening the elder man would be occupied with law books and papers.

Therefore the lad strolled out into the yard. His studying was done; and even if it had not been he was in no frame of mind to attack it to-night. A myriad of schemes and problems occupied his thought. Slowly he turned into the walk and presently he found himself in the street.

It was a still October twilight,—so still that one could hear the rustle of the dry leaves as they dropped from the trees and blew idly along the sidewalk. There was a tang of smoke in the air, and a blue haze from smoldering bonfires veiled the fall atmosphere.

Aimlessly Paul lingered. No one was in sight. Then the metallic shrillness of a bicycle bell broke the silence. He wheeled about. Noiselessly threading his way down the village highway came a thick-set, rosy-faced boy of sixteen or seventeen years of age.

"Hi, Carter!" called Paul. "Hold on! I want to see you."

Carter grinned; stopping his wheel by rising erect on its pedals, he vaulted to the ground.

"What's up, Paul?"

Without introduction Paul plunged into his subject. He spoke earnestly and with boyish eloquence.

"Say, Cart, what do you think of '20 starting a school paper?"

"A paper! Great hat, Kipper—what for?"

Kipper was Paul's nickname.

"Why, to read, man."

"Oh, don't talk of reading," was Melville Carter's spirited retort. "Aren't we all red-eyed already with Latin and Roman history? Why add a paper to our troubles?"

Paul did not reply.

"What do you want with a paper, Kipper?" persisted Melville.

"Why to print our life histories and obituaries in," he answered. "To extol our friends and damn our enemies."

Carter laughed.

"Come off," returned he, affectionately knocking Paul's hat down over his eyes.

"Stop your kidding, Cart. I'm serious."

"You really want a newspaper, Kip? *Another newspaper!* Scott! I don't. I never read the ones there are already."

"I don't mean a newspaper, Cart," explained Paul with a touch of irritation. "I mean a zippy little monthly with all the school news in it—hockey, football, class meetings, and all the things we'd like to read. Not highbrow stuff."

"Oh! I get you, Kipper," replied young Carter, a gleam of interest dawning in his face.

"That wouldn't be half bad. A school paper!" he paused thoughtfully. "But the money, Kip—the money to back such a scheme? What about that?"

"We could take subscriptions."

"At how much a subscrip, oh promoter?"

"I don't know," Paul responded vaguely. "One—twenty-five per—"

"Per—*haps*," cut in Melville, "and perhaps not. Who do you think, Kipper, is going to pay a perfectly good dollar and a quarter for the privilege of seeing his name in print and reading all the things he knew before?"

In spite of himself Paul chuckled.

"Maybe they wouldn't know them before."

"Football and hockey! Nix! Don't they all go to the games?"

"Not always. Besides, we'd put other things in—grinds on the Freshies—all sorts of stuff."

"I say! That wouldn't be so worse, would it?" declared Melville with appreciation.

He looked down and began to dig a hole in the earth with the toe of his much worn sneaker.

"Your idea is all right, Kip—corking," he asserted at length. "But the ducats—where would those come from? It would cost a pile to print a paper."

"I suppose we couldn't buy a press second-hand and do our own printing," ruminated Paul.

"Buy a press!" shouted Carter, breaking into a guffaw. "You are a green one, Kip, even if you are class president. Why, man alive, a printing press that's any good costs a small fortune—more money than the whole High School has, all put together. I know what presses cost because my father is in the publishing business."

Paul sighed.

"That's about what my dad said," he affirmed reluctantly. "He suggested we get someone to print the paper for us."

"Oh, we could do that all right if we had the spondulics."

"The subscriptions would net us quite a sum."

"How much could we bank on?"

"I've no idea," Paul murmured.

"I'll bet I could nail most of the Juniors. I'd simply stand them up against the wall and tell them it was their money or their life—death or a subscription to the—what are you going to call this rich and rare newspaper?" he inquired, suddenly breaking off in the midst of his harangue and turning to his companion.

"I hadn't got as far as that," answered Paul blankly.

"But you've got to get a name, you know," Melville declared. "You can't expect to boom something so hazy that it isn't called anything at all. *Don't you want to take our class paper* won't draw the crowd. You've got to start with a slogan—something spectacular and thrilling. *Buy the Nutcracker! Subscribe to the Fire-eater! Have a copy of the Jabberwock!* For goodness sake, christen it something! Start out with a punch or you'll never get anywhere. Why not call it *The March Hare*? That's wild and crazy enough to suit anybody. Then you can publish any old trash in it that you chose. They've brought it on themselves if they stand for such a title."

"The March Hare!" he repeated with enthusiasm. *"You've hit it, Cart!"*

Paul clapped a hand on his friend's shoulder.

"*The March Hare!*" he repeated with enthusiasm. "You've hit it, Cart! *The March Hare* it is! We'll begin getting subscriptions to-morrow."

"You wouldn't want to issue a sample copy first, would you?" Melville suggested.

"No, siree! That'll be the fun. They must go it blind. We'll make the whole thing as spooky and mysterious as we can. Nobody shall know what he is going to eat. It will be twice the sport."

"But suppose after you've collected all your money you find you can't get any one to print the paper?"

"We'll have to take a chance," replied Paul instantly. "If worst comes to worst we can give the money back again. But I shan't figure on doing that. We'll win out, Cart; don't you worry."

"Bully for you, old man! You sure are a sport. Nothing like selling something that doesn't even exist! I see you years hence on Wall Street, peddling nebulous gold mines and watered stocks."

"Oh, shut up, can't you!" laughed Paul good-naturedly. "Quit your joshing! I'm serious. You've got to help me, too. You must start in landing subscriptions to-morrow."

"I! I go around rooting for your *March Hare* when I know that not a line of it has seen printer's ink!" sniffed Melville.

"Sure!"

Melville grinned.

"Well, you have a nerve!" he affirmed.

"You're going to do it just the same, Cart."

There was a compelling, magnetic quality in Paul Cameron which had won for him his leadership at school; it came to his aid in the present instance.

Melville looked for a second into his chum's face and then smiled.

"All right," he answered. "I'm with you, Kipper. We'll see what we can do toward fooling the public."

"I don't mean to fool them," Paul retorted. "I'm in dead earnest. I mean to get out a good school paper that shall be worth the money people pay for it. There shall be no fake about it. To-morrow I shall call a class meeting and we'll elect an editorial staff—editor-in-chief, publicity committee, board of managers, and all the proper dignitaries. Then we'll get right down to work."

Melville regarded his friend with undisguised admiration.

"You'll make it a go, Kip!" he cried. "I feel it in my bones now. Hurrah for the *March Hare*! I can hear the shekels chinking into our pockets this minute. Put me down for the first subscription. I'll break the ginger-ale bottle over the treasury."

"Shall it be a dollar, a dollar and a quarter, or an out and out one-fifty?"

"Oh, put it at one-fifty. We're all millionaires and we may as well go in big while we're at it. What is one-fifty for such a ream of wisdom as we're going to get for our money?"

Melville vaulted into his bicycle saddle.

"Well, I'm off, Kipper," he called over his shoulder. "Got to do some errands for the Mater. So long!"

"I can depend on you, Cart?"

"Sure you can. I'll shout for your *March Hare* with all my lungs. I'm quite keen about it already."

Paul watched him speed through the gathering shadows and disappear round the turn in the road. Then, straightening his shoulders with resolution, he went into the house to seek his pillow and dream dreams of the *March Hare*.

CHAPTER II

THE CLASS MEETING AND WHAT FOLLOWED IT

The following day at recess, after a noisy clamor of conversation and laughter, the class meeting came to order.

"I have called you together to-day," began Paul Cameron from the platform, "to lay before 1920 a new undertaking. I am sure there is not one of you who does not want to make our class a unique and illustrious one. The Burmingham High School has never had a paper. 1920 has the great opportunity to give it one and to go down to history as its founder."

He paused.

"The big dailies do not appreciate us. They never write us up. Why should we not write ourselves up—chronicle our doings, that such noteworthy deeds may never be forgotten?"

A ripple of laughter greeted the interrogation.

Paul saw his advantage and went on. He painted in glowing terms his dream of the *March Hare*. Every instant the interest and enthusiasm of his audience increased. Once a storm of clapping broke in upon his words but he raised his hand and the noise ceased. Quietly he closed his modest speech with the suggestion that a managing board be appointed to put the project into operation, if such were the pleasure of the meeting. Before he could seat himself a dozen boys were on their feet.

"Mr. President!" shouted Melville Carter.

"Mr. President!" came at the same moment from Donald Hall.

"Mr. President! Mr. President!" The cry rang from every corner of the room.

Paul listened to each speaker in turn.

1920 was not only unanimous but insistent upon the new venture.

In less time than it takes to tell it Paul himself was elected editor-in-chief, an editorial staff had been appointed, Melville Carter was voted in as business manager, and Billie Ransome as publicity agent. Nor did 1920's fervor end there. Before the meeting adjourned every person in the class had not only pledged himself to subscribe to the *March Hare* but had promised to get one or more outside subscriptions.

Paul, descending from the speaker's desk, was the center of an admiring and eager group of students.

"I say, Kip, where are you going to get the paper printed?" questioned Donald Hall.

"I don't know yet," replied Paul jauntily.

"We'll have to see how much money we are going to have."

"Why don't you get Mel Carter's father to do it? He publishes the *Echo*, and Mel is our business manager. That ought to give us some pull."

Paul started.

"I never thought of asking Mr. Carter," he returned slowly. "I don't believe Melville did, either. He's kind of a grouch. Still, he couldn't do more than refuse. Of course the *Echo* is pretty highbrow. Mr. Carter might feel we were beneath his notice."

"No matter," was Donald's cheerful answer. "I guess we could live through it if he did sit on us. Besides, maybe he wouldn't. Perhaps he'd enjoy fostering young genius. You said you were going to make the paper worth while and something more than an athletic journal."

"Yes, I am," retorted Paul promptly. "We've got to make it tally up with what the subscribers pay for it. I mean to put in politics, poetry, philosophy, and every other sort of dope," he concluded with a smile.

"You certainly are the one and only great editor-in-chief!" chuckled Donald. Then he added hastily: "There's Melville now. Why don't you buttonhole him about his father?"

"I will," cried Paul, hurrying across the corridor to waylay his chum.

"Hi, Cart!"

Melville came to a stop.

"Say, what's the matter with your father printing the *March Hare* for us?"

"What!" The lad was almost speechless with astonishment.

"I say," repeated Paul earnestly, "what's the matter with your father printing the *March Hare*? He prints the *Echo*. Don't you believe he'd print our paper too?"

Melville was plainly disconcerted.

"I—I—don't know," he managed to stammer uneasily. "You see, the *Echo* office is such a darn busy place. My father is driven most to death. Besides, we couldn't pay much. It wouldn't be worth the bother to the *Echo*."

"Maybe not," said Paul. "But don't you think if your father knew we were trying to run a decent paper he might like to help us out? Who knows but some of us may become distinguished journalists when we grow up? There may be real geniuses in our midst—celebrities."

"Great Scott, Paul, but you have got a wily tongue! You've kissed the Blarney Stone if ever man has!"

But Paul was not to be cajoled from his purpose.

"Won't you put it up to your Pater when you go home, Cart?"

"*I* ask him!" exclaimed Melville, drawing back a step or two. "I couldn't, Kip. Don't put me in such a hole. I wouldn't dare. Straight goods, I wouldn't. You don't know my dad. Why, he wouldn't even hear me out. He'd say at the outset that it was all rot and that he couldn't be bothered with such a scheme."

"You absolutely refuse to ask him?"

Melville turned a wretched face toward Paul.

"I'd do most anything for you, Kip," he said miserably. "You know that. But I couldn't ask favors of my father for you or anybody else. He isn't like other people. I'd go to any one else in a minute. But Father's so—well, it would just take more nerve than I've got. He's all right, though. Don't think he isn't. It's only that he's pretty stiff. I'm afraid of him; straight goods, I am."

Paul nodded.

"I see."

There was an awkward pause.

"Would you have any objection to somebody else going to him?"

"You?"

"Possibly."

"Not the least in the world," Melville declared. "I don't see why you shouldn't if you want to take a chance. You'll have no luck, though."

"He couldn't any more than kick me out."

"He'll do that all right!" Melville exclaimed, with a grin.

"What if he does?" asked the editor-in-chief with a shrug of his shoulders.

"Well, if you don't mind being turned down and swept out of the office before your mouth is fairly open, go ahead."

"I shan't go to the office," responded Paul deliberately. "I shall go around to the house."

"Good heavens!"

"Why not?"

"Well, I don't know why—only it makes Father as mad as hops to be disturbed about business after he gets home."

"I'm not supposed to know that, am I?"

"N—o."

"Then I shall come to the house," reiterated Paul firmly. "Your father will have more leisure there and I think he will be more likely to listen."

"He won't listen to you anywhere."

"We'll see whether he will or not," said Paul. "At least I can make my try and convince myself."

"It'll be no use, Kip," persisted Melville. "I hate to have you disappointed, old chap."

"I shan't be disappointed," said Paul kindly. "I shan't allow myself to expect much. Even if your father does turn me down he may give me a useful pointer or two."

"He won't do anything for you," Melville asserted dubiously. "He'll just have nothing to do with it."

In spite of Paul's optimism he was more than half of Melville's opinion.

Mr. Carter was well known throughout Burmingham as a stern, austere man whom people feared rather than loved. He had the reputation of being shrewd, close-fisted, and sharp at a bargain,—a person of few friends and many enemies. He was a great fighter, carrying a grudge to any length for the sheer pleasure of gratifying it. Therefore many a more mature and courageous promoter than Paul Cameron had shrunk from approaching him with a business proposition.

Even Paul did not at all relish the mission before him; he was, however, too manly to shirk it. Hence that evening, directly after dinner, he made his way to the mansion of Mr. Arthur Presby Carter, the wealthy owner of the *Echo*, Burmingham's most widely circulated daily.

Fortunately or unfortunately—Paul was uncertain which—the capitalist was at home and at leisure; and with beating heart the boy was ushered into the presence of this illustrious gentleman.

Mr. Carter greeted him politely but with no cordiality.

"So you're Paul Cameron. I've had dealings with your father," he remarked dryly. "What can I do for you?"

Paul's courage ebbed. The question was crisp and direct, demanding a reply of similar tenor. With a gulp of apprehension the lad struggled to make an auspicious opening for his subject; but no words came to his tongue.

"Perhaps you brought a message from your father," suggested the great man, after he had waited impatiently for an interval.

"No, sir. Father didn't know that I was coming," Paul contrived to stammer. "I came on my own account. I wanted to know if you wouldn't like to print the *March Hare*, a new monthly publication that is soon coming out."

"The *March Hare*!" repeated Mr. Carter incredulously.

Paul nodded silently.

"Did I hear aright?" inquired Mr. Carter majestically. "Did you say the *March Hare*?"

The title took on a ludicrous incongruity as it fell from his lips.

"Yes, sir," gasped Paul. "We are going to get out a High School paper and call it the *March Hare*."

Mr. Carter made no comment. He seemed too stunned with amazement to do so.

"We want to make it a really good paper," went on Paul desperately. "The school has never had a paper before, but I don't see why it shouldn't. We're all studying English and writing compositions. Why shouldn't we write something for publication?"

"Why, indeed!"

There was a note of sarcasm, or was it ridicule, in the words, that put Paul on his mettle.

"We intend to make it a good, dignified magazine," he went on quickly. "We plan to have the school news and some more serious articles in it. We've got a managing board, and an editorial staff, and all the things papers have."

"And why do you come to me?"

"Because we need a printer."

"You wish me to print this remarkable document?"

Paul smiled ingenuously. "Yes, sir." There was a silence. Mr. Carter seemed too dumfounded to speak.

"You see," went on the boy, "getting out a paper would give us fellows some business experience and at the same time some practice in writing. I believe we could make the thing pay, too."

"How many subscribers have you?"

"I had two last night—myself and another boy," Paul replied. "But to-day I have a hundred and fifty; by to-morrow I expect to add about two hundred more."

"Your circulation increases rapidly," remarked Mr. Carter, the shadow of a smile on his face.

"Yes, sir, it does," came innocently from Paul.

"How many numbers would you wish to issue annually?"

"Ten. We'd want to bring out a paper the first of each month from October to June. With our studies, that would be about all we could handle, I guess."

"I guess so, too," agreed Mr. Carter caustically.

"How large a paper do you plan to have?" he added an instant later.

"Oh, I hadn't thought much about that. It would depend on how much space we could fill up. Perhaps twenty-five pages."

The magnate nodded.

It was impossible to fathom what was going on in his mind. Was he preparing to burst into a tirade of ridicule, or was he really considering the proposition?

"We'd want some good sort of a cover, of course," Paul put in as an afterthought.

"In colors, I suppose."

"Yes, sir."

"And nice paper and clear print."

"Yes, indeed," said Paul, not noting the increasing sarcasm in the man's voice.

"How much would you charge for an annual subscription?"

"A dollar and a half."

"Have you any idea what it would cost to get out a paper such as you propose?" There was a ring of contempt in the words.

"No, sir."

"Well, it would cost a good deal more money than you have to offer, young man." With a cruel satisfaction he saw the boy's face fall.

"Then that's the end of it, I guess, so far as your firm is concerned," replied Paul, turning toward the door. "I'll have to take my proposition somewhere else."

Something in the boy's proud bearing appealed to the man. It had not dawned on him until now that the lad actually considered the proposal a strictly business one. He had thought that he came to wheedle and beg, and Mr. Carter detested having favors asked of him. Calling Paul back, he motioned him to sit down.

"I'm not ready to wind up this matter quite so quickly," he observed. "Let us talk the thing over a little more fully. Suppose I were to make you a proposition."

Leaning forward, he took a cigar from the library table and, lighting it, puffed a series of rings into the air.

"There are certain things that I want to do in Burmingham," he announced in leisurely fashion. There was a twinkle of humor beneath the shaggy brows. "Your father, for example, doesn't take the *Echo*. He has none too cordial feeling toward me personally, and in addition he says my paper is too conservative. Then there are firms that I can't get to advertise with us—business houses in the town that are not represented on our pages. And lastly, Judge Damon has constantly refused to do a set of political articles for me. Put those deals through for me, and I'll print your *March Hare*."

He leaned back in his chair, regarding Paul with a provoking smile.

"But how can I?" gasped Paul, bewildered.

Mr. Carter shrugged his shoulders.

"That's up to you," he said. "Sometimes fools rush in where angels fear to tread. Your father, for instance, will certainly want this venture of yours to succeed. Tell him that if he takes the *Echo* instead of the *Mirror*, or in addition to it, it will be a big help to you."

"But my father—" burst out Paul, then stopped suddenly.

"I know he doesn't like me," put in Mr. Carter calmly. "We differ in politics and we've had one bad set-to on the subject. He won't take my paper—wouldn't do it for love or money. I know perfectly well how he feels."

"So that's why you want to make him do it?"

"Never you mind, sonny. I want you to get him to. That's enough," was the curt retort.

Paul flushed.

"And with regard to the advertising I mentioned," continued Mr. Carter, "I am sure you can easily carry that through. The Kimball and Dalrymple boys are in your class, aren't they?"

"Yes, sir."

"Tell them the *Echo* wants an ad. from the firm of George L. Kimball and from Dalrymple and Company."

"Oh!"

"As for Judge Damon—well, if you can't manage the judge, I can't tell you how to do it. All is, I want six articles on The League of Nations. He's an authority on international law and the best man I know to handle the subject. He hasn't, however, much more use for me than your father has, and thus far has politely refused every offer I've made him."

"Carl Damon is on our *March Hare* literary staff," ventured Paul.

"There you are!" declared Mr. Carter triumphantly. "Set him at his father's heels and tell him to bring me the six articles I'm after. Then you boys flax round and get me ten new firms to advertise in the *Echo* and I'll sign a contract with you to print your *March Hare* in good shape."

The lips of the elder man curled humorously.

Paul rose.

"It's mighty good of you, sir," he murmured.

"Don't thank me, youngster, until you've landed your bargain," protested Mr. Carter with shame-faced haste. "Remember I said that when you had fulfilled my conditions *then* I would print your *March Hare*; I shan't do it until then."

"But I am sure we can fulfill them."

"You seem very certain of it."

"I feel so."

"Humph! Have you ever tried to get an ad?"

"No, sir."

"Or asked your father why he didn't take the *Echo*?"

"No."

"Or tried to worm an article out of Judge Damon?"

Paul shook his head.

"Then you've some fun ahead of you," remarked Mr. Carter, rising. "I'd wait to do my crowing if I were you."

With a grim laugh and a gesture of farewell he swept the boy from the room.

CHAPTER III

MR. CAMERON TAKES A HAND IN THE GAME

As Paul walked down the steps of the Carter mansion he felt, as did David Copperfield in the presence of the waiter, very young indeed. Had Mr. Carter simply been making game of him? And was the business world actually such a network of schemes and complexities?

And how did it happen that the printing of a newspaper was such a difficult and expensive undertaking? Why should it be?

Paper and ink were common enough commodities surely. All that had to be done was to print, and if a press were at hand it must be the easiest thing in the world to do that. Why did people make such a fuss over printing a paper?

Thoughtfully he walked home and turned in at his own door.

He was in a very sober frame of mind, unwontedly sober for him; so sober, in fact, that his father, whom he encountered in the hall, exclaimed:

"Goodness me, son, you look as if your last friend on earth had perished. What's the matter?"

The boy smiled faintly.

"Nothing, sir."

"But you'd never look like that if there weren't. Come, tell me all about it. What's the trouble?"

The gray eyes of the man regarded the lad kindly.

"I'm—I'm just thinking."

"About what, pray? Something pretty solemn, I'll be bound," persisted his father.

"Oh, I've a lot of things on my mind," answered Paul hesitatingly.

"Suppose you give me a sample of one of them."

"Just business," replied Paul.

As the words fell with familiar cadence, Mr. Cameron laughed. How often he had met his wife's troubled inquiries with the same retort.

"Business, eh! And how long is it since the burdens of business have fallen on your young shoulders?"

"Since yesterday."

"And already you are bowed to the earth with worry?" commented his father playfully. "Come, son, what's troubling you?"

"The school paper."

"Not going to be able to put it through?"

"Oh, it's not that," said Paul quickly. "We are going to put it through all right, although at this moment I don't exactly see how. I had no idea it cost so much to get a paper printed."

"It isn't the actual printing, so much as the typesetting and all that goes with it, that makes printing an expensive job," explained Mr. Cameron. "Just now, too, paper and ink cost a great deal, and labor is high."

"Did people always have to pay so much for paper?"

"People didn't always use to have paper, my son."

Paul opened his eyes.

"What did they print on, then?"

"They didn't have printing presses, either," answered Mr. Cameron. "Long ago people did not care so much for reading as we do now. Most of them hadn't education enough to read a book or a paper if they had had one. In fact, many kings, bishops, and persons of rank could neither read nor write. Charlemagne could not sign his own name. The era before the Renaissance was an age of unbelievable ignorance. It is a marvel that with the turmoil of war and the utter lack of interest in anything intellectual any learning came out of the period."

"But aren't there very old writings in some of the museums?"

"Yes, we have manuscripts of very ancient date," agreed his father. "Much of the matter in them however—material such as the Norse Sagas and the Odes of Horace—were handed down by word of mouth and were not written until long after they had been chanted or sung. Poets and minstrels passed on their tales to other bards; had they not done so, Homer, Ossian, and the Sanscrit Vedas would have been lost to us. A metric arrangement of the stories was probably made to aid the singers in remembering their subject matter. You know how much easier it is to memorize something that has a swing or rhythm?"

Paul nodded.

"That without question accounts for the poetic form in which some of our oldest literature has come down to us," Mr. Cameron said. "Then, as good luck would have it, Roman and Greek slaves were compelled to copy many of the writings of the time on long rolls of vellum or papyrus, and in that way more of the ancient literature was preserved. There was only a small reading public in either Rome or Greece, and those who were interested in books could secure what they wished through professional scribes, or could listen to readings of the classics from the portico of some rich nobleman who had been fortunate enough to secure a copy of some rare poem or play. Often, too, such things were read in the baths, which in those days took the place of our modern clubs."

"And that was the way we got our early books?"

"Yes. There were slaves whose duty it was to do nothing but copy manuscripts for their masters. They were given food, shelter, and clothing in return for their labors. Of course they were not an educated class of workers, and in consequence they often made mistakes; but they served to prevent the total destruction of such classics as—"

"Cæsar's Commentaries, I suppose," interrupted Paul mischievously.

"Cæsar's writings would have been a great loss," declared his father good-humoredly.

"Not to me! Nor Cicero's either."

"But are they not all old and interesting as a relic of history?"

"They are more interesting now that you have told me something about them," admitted Paul, with characteristic honesty.

"Oh, you would find many interesting and even amusing incidents connected with these early writings, were you to study into the matter," continued Mr. Cameron. "Fancy, for example, a hand-written scroll of a book selling for the equivalent of two cents in our money; and fancy others not selling at all, and being used by grocers to wrap up spices and pastries. The modern author thinks he is paid little enough. What, I wonder, would he say to such treatment?"

Paul laughed.

"Even at a later date when the monks began copying and illuminating manuscripts there was at first no great demand for them. Learning was conceded to be the rightful possession of the rich and powerful, and whether the kings or nobles of the court could read or not, most of the books were bought by them simply as art works. Many, of course, especially the most skillfully illuminated ones, were very beautiful and were well worth owning."

"But think of the time it must have taken to make them by hand!" speculated Paul.

"Time was no object in those days," smiled his father. "There was nothing to hurry about. A monk would toil at a single manuscript day after day, month after month; sometimes year after year. It must have been a sleepy, tiresome business to write out even a short manuscript so carefully, to say nothing of a long one like the Bible. What wonder that the patient workers were so glad when their tedious task was done that they inscribed at the end of it a little song of thanksgiving. I remember seeing one old book in a European museum at the end of which was written:

"This book was illuminated, bound, and perfected by Henry Cremer, vicar of the Collegiate Church of Saint Stephen in Metz, on the Feast of the Assumption of the Blessed Virgin, in the year of our Lord 1456.

"Thanks be to God, Hallelujah!'

"No doubt the pious Henry Cremer was thankful for many other things besides the completion of his manuscript, but I am sure he must have been human enough to draw a sigh of relief when he put the last stroke to such a tedious piece of work. Don't you think so?"

"I'll bet he was," agreed Paul.

"Can't you see those patient monks alone in their dimly lighted cells, silently writing day after day?" continued Mr. Cameron. "Many a poor fellow who drudged so mechanically at his task copied the errors in the text quite as faithfully as the rest of it. In consequence, it at last became imperative to demand that the scribes work with more intelligence, and therefore at the end of a manuscript would be such an admonition as this:

> *"I adjure thee who shall transcribe this book by our Lord Jesus Christ, and by His glorious coming to judge the quick and the dead, that thou compare what thou transcribest and correct it carefully according to the copy from which thou transcribest, and that thou also annex a copy of this adjuration to what thou hast written.'*

"Thus, you see, was the copyist forced to study his text and pass the caution against mistakes on to others. Nevertheless, solemn and reverent as was this warning, it did not prevent errors from slipping into the old illuminated manuscripts, and many a one is marred by misspelling or miswording."

"I don't wonder it is," exclaimed Paul. "Why, the very thought that I must not make a mistake would cause me to make one. Besides, I should get so sleepy after I had written for hours that I should not know what I was doing."

"Probably much of the time they didn't."

Paul thought a moment.

"I suppose, though, the monks were paid for their hard work, so it was only fair for them to be careful," he reflected.

"On the contrary," replied his father, "they were not paid any more than were the slaves whom the Greeks and Romans employed. Their living was given them; that was all. Often the books they made were very beautiful and were sold to dignitaries of the Church or to titled persons for great sums; but any monies received from such a transaction went into the coffers of the Church and not into the monks' pockets. The Church however, in return, provided them with all they needed so they did not go entirely unrewarded. Some day when we can find time we will go to the city and hunt up some of these rare old manuscripts in the museum. You would be interested to see how exquisitely many of them are done. The initial letter, or frequently the catch word, is painted in color, and the borders are richly decorated with intricate scroll-work."

"Did the monks have to design the pages as well as print them?" inquired Paul with surprise.

"The same monk did not always do all the work," his father said. "Some merely inscribed the text and illuminated the first letter or word; afterward the sheets were handed to some one else who designed the decoration and sketched it in. Then it went to the colorist, who in turn illuminated, or painted, the drawing. You will find every inch of some of the more ornate manuscripts filled in with designs. The great objection to this method was that several persons handled the work and therefore in many cases the decoration had no relation whatsoever to the text; in fact, frequently it was entirely inappropriate to it."

Paul smiled.

"No more relation, I suppose, than the text of our school paper will have to its name: *March Hare*."

"Just about the same," conceded his father with amusement. "So that's the title you've selected for your monthly?"

"Yes, sir. We couldn't seem to think of anything better."

"It's not bad at all. How are you coming with the project? You seem bothered."

"I am—a little."

"What's the matter? Haven't you money enough to induce anybody to print your publication?"

"Oh, I have a printer," replied Paul confidently. "The *Echo* is going to get it out for us."

"The *Echo*!" Mr. Cameron regarded the lad incredulously.

"Yes, sir."

"But—but—how in the name of goodness did you pull off a bargain like that?" demanded the man. "The *Echo* of all people! Why, I should as soon think of asking the government to do it! Their rates are enormous and they never take outside work. Are you quite sure they have agreed to do it?"

"Yes. There's no mistake about it, Dad. They were perfectly serious. They made a few conditions, though."

"Whom did you see?"

"Mr. Carter."

"Carter! Mr. Carter himself? Mr. Arthur Carter?"

"Yes."

"My soul and body!" murmured Mr. Cameron. "I wouldn't have believed he'd see you. You did have a nerve, son! Why, nobody ever asks a favor of Carter. I wouldn't, for a thousand dollars. It's a marvel he listened to you. And he is actually going to print your paper?"

"Yes, sir—that is, under certain conditions." Paul waited an instant, then added dryly: "In fact, Dad, you're one of the conditions."

"I!"

The boy chuckled.

"Uh-huh. He wants you to subscribe to the *Echo*."

"He does, does he!" Mr. Cameron cried with indignation. "The impertinence of the man! Well, he can continue to want me to. When he finds me doing it he will be years older than he is now. What does he think? Does he expect to turn me from a broad-minded Democrat into a stand-pat Republican like himself? The old fox! He just enjoyed sending me that message, and by my own son, too. I ran against him for Mayor in 1916 and lost the fight because I wouldn't use the weapons he did. You were a little chap then and so do not remember much about it; but it was a nasty business. Since that day we've never spoken. Take his paper! I wouldn't so much as look at it if he offered it to me free of charge on a silver salver."

Paul regarded his father with consternation.

"But I say, Dad, if you don't help us out, it's all up with the *March Hare*."

"I can't help that," blustered Mr. Cameron, striding impatiently across the hall. "Why, it's preposterous! He's making a goat of you, son, that's all. He never meant to print your paper. He simply made up a lot of conditions that he knew could never be fulfilled and sent you away with them. It was a mean trick. Just like him, too! He'd think it a great joke."

"I don't believe he was joking," Paul answered slowly. "And anyway, even if he were, I don't have to take it as a joke. I can take him seriously, fulfill his contract, and make him live up to his agreement, can't I? Then if the whole thing were a joke, the joke would be on him."

Mr. Cameron gazed into the boy's eager face a few seconds, then smiled suddenly.

"That's not a bad idea," he observed. "We'd have Carter fast in his own trap then."

"To be sure."

"By Jove, Paul—if I haven't half a mind to help you out!" He slapped his son on the shoulder. "I'll do it! I declare if I won't. I'll send in my subscription to the *Echo* to-morrow. I needn't read the thing, even if I do take it. What other tasks did the old schemer impose on you?"

"I've got to get some ads for him—ten of them."

"Whew!"

"And I've got to ask Judge Damon for six articles on The League of Nations."

"Ha, ha! That's a good one," chuckled Mr. Cameron. "The League of Nations is like a red rag to the Judge. He can't be trusted to speak of it, let alone writing about it."

"Mr. Carter said Judge Damon was an expert on international law," explained Paul.

"So he is, so he is! But he isn't expressing his opinion of The League of Nations, just the same."

"You think he wouldn't do the articles?"

"Do them? Mercy, no!"

"Then I guess it was all a joke," murmured Paul, with a wistful, disappointed quiver of the lip.

Mr. Cameron saw the joyousness fade from the young face.

"It was contemptible for him to put up such a game on you kids!" he ejaculated.

Thrusting his hands into his pockets he stared up at the ceiling.

"I'm not so sure," he presently remarked slowly, "but what, if your uncle knew the circumstances, he might be coaxed into meeting Carter's demand."

"Do you think so?"

Again courage shone in Paul's eyes.

"I'm pretty sure of it."

The lad's brow became radiant.

"I'll see Damon myself," went on Cameron humorously. "I'll tell him I have yielded up my preferences for the common good and that he must do the same. His son Carl is in your class, isn't he?"

"Yes, sir."

"Then it's as much his duty to help on 1920 as mine. He adores that boy of his. You leave him to me. I'll bring him round to our way of thinking all right."

"And the ads?"

"Set your classmates on their fathers," was the terse reply as the elder man clapped on his hat and left the house.

Paul watched him out of sight, then sighed a happy little sigh of satisfaction. With such a sympathetic colleague to fall back upon he felt confident the *March Hare* would succeed.

CHAPTER IV

ANOTHER ALLY

Mr. Cameron was as good as his word.

The next morning when Paul appeared at breakfast, he was greeted with the words: "Well, I won Damon over. You're to go around there this evening and he'll have a paper ready for you to the effect that in consideration of the *Echo* printing the *March Hare*, the judge will write for the *Echo* six articles on the pros and cons of The League of Nations. You are to get Carter to sign this agreement and then we'll lock it up in my strong box at the bank."

"That's bully, Dad. It was mighty good of you to take this trouble for us."

"That's all right, son. I'm always glad to help you boys out. Besides," he added whimsically, "I am not entirely philanthropic. The thing amuses me. I always enjoy beating Carter when I get the chance."

Paul regarded his father affectionately. The big man seemed very human just at that moment,—little more, in fact, than a boy like himself.

"Then, as I understand it, all we fellows have to do now is to round up the ten ads.," he said, dropping into his chair at the table and vigorously attacking his grape-fruit.

"What ads. are you talking about, Paul?" asked his mother, who had just entered the room.

"Oh, we boys down at school want to get some ads. to help publish our new paper."

Mrs. Cameron listened while the plans of the *March Hare* were unfolded to her.

"Hill and Holden, the Garden Street grocers, are going to put a new coffee on the market; their man told me about it yesterday and said they were going to advertise it very extensively."

"There's your chance, Paul!" cried Mr. Cameron. "Call them up this minute and nail them before they send the advertisement to the papers. We're customers of theirs and without doubt they'd just as soon send their announcement to the *Echo* through you. Tell them they will be doing a service to the High School pupils, most of whose families' names are on their books."

Paul needed no second bidding. He sprang to the telephone. A few instants later he re-entered the room with sparkling eyes.

"O. K.!" he said. "I talked with one of the firm who said they would be glad to help us out. They'll prepare the ad. and let me have it to-morrow. They want a quarter of a page."

"They do? Well, well, Paul! That should net the *Echo* something," Mr. Cameron remarked. "If all the boys' mothers help them as yours has, your *March Hare* will be a certainty by to-morrow."

"You were a brick, Mater."

"I just happened to recall hearing the man speak of it," returned Mrs. Cameron.

Nevertheless it was quite evident that she was pleased to aid her boy.

"You don't remember happening to hear any one else mention advertising, do you, my dear?" asked her husband.

"I'm afraid not," was his wife's laughing reply.

"Don't tease Mater, Dad," said Paul. "She's done her bit. May the others do as well."

Rising from breakfast, he bent and kissed his mother affectionately.

"I'm off to school!" he called. "I shall put this advertising stunt up to the business manager. He's got to expect to have something to do."

"That's right, Paul," returned Mr. Cameron approvingly. "The clever business man is the one who organizes his affairs and then throws at least a part of the responsibility of carrying them out on the men in his employ. Nobody is ever interested in an undertaking in which he has no part. Share your work with the other fellow if you want to get the best out of him. Put it on his shoulders and make him feel that you expect him to do it—that you trust him to do it. He'll do ten times as much for you and he will pull with you—not against you. We're all human and like to be important. Remember that in handling men. It is one of the great secrets of success. Now off with you! You'll be late if you stand here philosophizing."

Away scampered Paul. A moment later his wheel was crunching over the blue gravel of the driveway and speeding down the macadam road. Soon he was in the classroom.

Excitement ran high that morning. What Cæsar did in Gaul, what Cyrus and the Silician Queen had to say to one another was of far less import to the agitated students than what the Class of 1920 did that day in Burmingham. Nevertheless the recitations dragged on somehow and by and by the geometries, Roman histories, and the peregrinations of Cyrus were tucked into the desks, and the staff of the *March Hare* got together for a hurried business meeting in the corridor.

The boys were enthusiastic that Paul had found a printer.

"Hurrah for you, Kipper!" they shouted.

"Good work, old man!"

"Leave it to Kip!" they cried in chorus.

"You'll have to get the ads.," announced Paul. "I've secured one. I leave the rest of them to you."

"Right-o! We'll 'tend to them," piped Donald Hall with assurance.

"My father's firm has never advertised," declared Dave Chandler. "I'll put it up to Pater when I get home."

"My uncle will help us out; I bet he will," promised Oscar Hamilton. "Robey and Hamilton, you know."

"The more the merrier," responded Paul gayly. "Just call me up this evening and tell me what luck you've had."

"Sure, old fellow! We'll do that!" came from the boys as they dispersed.

The remainder of the morning Paul mingled fragments of chemistry and Greek with visions of the *March Hare*, and the moment school was out he dashed home to complete his studying and get it out of the way that he might be free to go to see Judge Damon directly after dinner.

Despite the dignity of his profession the judge was a much less formidable person to face than Mr. Arthur Presby Carter. He was a simple, kindly man, with an ingratiating smile and a keen sympathy with human nature. He was, moreover, very fond of young people. He liked all boys, seeming never to forget the fact that he himself had been one of them not so many years ago.

Therefore, no sooner had Paul presented himself at the front door than he was shown into the study where, before a bright fire blazing on the hearth, the judge sat smoking.

"Come in, Paul," he called cordially. "Your father told me

about this undertaking of yours, and I hear I am to be one of your victims."

"I'm afraid you are, sir."

"Well, well! I suppose doing what we do not enjoy is good for our characters," returned the judge mischievously. "If you boys propose to do some serious writing of English and secure a little business experience, certainly your aim is a worthy one and we older folks should back you up. It's a far more sensible vent for your energy, to my mind, than so much football."

"Oh, we're not going to give over our football, sir," asserted Paul with prompt candor.

"No, indeed! Keep up your games by all means. But moderation is a jewel. A little football goes a good way, while business training is never amiss."

"We expect to get quite a bit of business training out of issuing our paper," said Paul modestly.

"And in order to do it, you young rascals are going to rope me into your schemes, are you?" demanded the judge.

"Mr. Carter is."

"It's the same thing—or rather it isn't the same thing, for what I would not consent to do for Mr. Carter I am going to do for you boys."

Paul murmured his thanks.

"Tut, tut! Say no more about it," Judge Damon commanded hastily. "My son is in the class, you know; surely I should be showing little loyalty to 1920 if I were not ready to help make it glorious; and even if I had no boy in the High School it would be the same. I should be glad to promote so worthy an undertaking."

From the litter of papers on the desk the man took up a crisp white sheet which he folded carefully and slipped into an envelope.

"There is a legal contract for Mr. Carter to sign," he said. "It states that in consideration of the *Echo* Press printing ten numbers of the *March Hare*, I am to furnish Mr. Carter with six articles on the League of Nations."

"It's mighty good of you, sir."

The judge waved his hand.

"Don't let the favor oppress you, sonny," he said. "Along with your father I am having my little joke on Carter. I'd like to see his face when you confront him with this bit of paper. He'll be bound to carry out his bargain whether he likes it or not."

"You don't think he'll back down."

"Carter back down! No, indeed. Mr. Carter is a man of his word. Although I differ from him on just about every possible subject, I am glad to give the devil his due. What he promises he will stick to; never fear," Judge Damon declared quickly.

This prediction proved to be no idle one for when, within two or three days, Paul presented himself once more in the library of Mr. Arthur Presby Carter and placed in that august person's hand not only the ten advertisements for the *Echo* but his father's subscription to the same paper, and the written agreement of the judge, Mr. Carter, although plainly chagrined, did not demur.

On the contrary he glanced keenly at the youthful diplomat, observing grimly:

"You are an enterprising young man, I will say that for you. I should not mind knowing to what methods you resorted to win these concessions from these stern-purposed gentlemen. Did you bribe or chloroform them?"

The boy laughed triumphantly.

"Neither, sir."

"The judge, for example—I can't imagine what influence

could have been brought to bear on him to have achieved such a result. I have offered him a good price for those articles and he has repeatedly refused it. And now he is going to do them for nothing."

"He just wanted to help us out."

"And your father?"

"He was game, too."

Mr. Carter was silent.

"Well, I guess I can be as good a sport as they can," he observed at length. "Get your material together for your first number of the *March Hare* and bring it over to the *Echo* office. I'll see that one of our staff gives you a lesson on how to get it into form. Have you a typewriter?"

"No, sir."

"Know how to run one?"

"No."

"That's unlucky. We don't like to handle copy that isn't typed. It's too hard on the eyes and takes us too long. However, we must make the best of it, I suppose. Only be sure to write plainly and on but one side of the paper; and do not fold or roll your sheets. That is one thing no publisher will stand for—rolled manuscript. Remember that."

"I will, sir."

"I guess that's all for now. Good night, youngster."

"Good night, sir."

Although the leave-taking was curt it was not unkind and Paul returned home with a feeling that in spite of what he had heard of Mr. Carter's character he neither feared nor disliked the gruff man; in fact, in the sharp-eyed visage there was actually something that appealed. To his surprise the lad found himself rather liking Mr. Carter.

CHAPTER V

PAUL GIVES THANKS FOR HIS BLESSINGS

When Paul came into the house that afternoon his father called to him from the little den off the hall.

"Come here a moment, son," he cried. "I've something to show you."

The boy hurried forward, all curiosity. He found his father seated before a desk on which was spread an old manuscript, brightened here and there by letters of blue or scarlet.

"Strangely enough, Mr. Jordan, the curio collector, was in my office to-day and had this treasure with him. When I mentioned that I should like to have you see it, immediately, in most generous fashion, he suggested that I bring it home and show it to you. It is almost priceless and of course I demurred; but he insisted. He had just bought it at an auction in New York and was, I fancy, glad to find some one who was interested and would appreciate it. It is not complete; if it were it would be very valuable. It is just a few stray sheets from an ancient psalter. Nevertheless its workmanship is exquisite and it is well worth owning. Notice the beautiful lettering."

Paul bent over the vellum pages. The manuscript, now spotted by age, was marvelously penned, being written evenly and with extreme care in Latin characters.

"Were all the old books written in Latin?" he inquired with surprise.

Mr. Cameron nodded.

"Yes, and not only were the first manuscripts and books phrased in Latin but most of the very early printed books were written in the same language," he answered. "In those days learning was not for the general public. There was no such spirit of democracy known as now exists. It cheapened a thing to have it within the reach of the vulgar herd. Even Horace, much as we honor him, once complained because some of his odes had strayed into the hands of the common people 'for whom they were not intended.' Books, in the olden time, were held to be for only the fortunate few. The educated class considered a little learning a dangerous thing. If the people got to know too much they were liable to become unruly and less easy to handle. Therefore books were kept out of their reach. In Germany there was even a large fine and the penalty of imprisonment imposed on any one who printed, published, or bought a book translated from the Latin or Greek unless such translation had previously been censored by the authorities. Hence the people who could not read the languages were entirely cut off from all literature."

"I never heard of such a thing!" exclaimed Paul indignantly.

"No, you never did, thank God! We live in an age and a country of freedom. But the world has not always been so easy or so comfortable a place to live in as it is now."

Mr. Cameron touched the manuscript before him daintily with his finger, betraying by the gesture the reverence of the true book-lover.

"This book," he remarked, "is, as you see, done on vellum. Most of the illuminators of ancient books preferred that material for their work. Papyrus such as the Romans used was too brittle to be folded or sewed, and therefore could not be bound into book form; it had to be rolled on rollers, and even then was liable to crack. It was far too perishable for bookmaking. Hence the old scribes turned to vellum, or sheepskin. But later, when the printing press came along, vellum became very unpopular indeed, because the grease in the skin spread the ink or else would not absorb it, and the harsh surface destroyed the type. Even had these difficulties not arisen, vellum would have had to be abandoned since the number of skins demanded for the making of a thick book was prohibitive. Imagine three hundred unlucky sheep offering up their skins in order to produce one of the first printed Bibles!"

"Great Scott!" Paul whistled, regarding his father with incredulity.

"I was as surprised as you when I read the statement," declared his father. "At that rate, where would the sheep be in a little while? All slaughtered and made into books. Fortunately the public of that day did not, as I have already explained, care much for reading; so perhaps that is the secret why some of the sheep were spared."

"Why didn't they print their books on paper?" inquired Paul thoughtlessly.

"Paper, you must remember, was not yet discovered; that is, it was unknown in western Europe. It had been in use in China, however, for some time; but China was not a generous country that spread its inventions to other lands. What the Chinese discovered they kept to themselves. Nor, in fact, was there any extended means of spreading such things except through the primitive methods of conquest or travel. Wars enough there were, it is true; but travel was very infrequent. Moreover, I seriously doubt if scribes would have used paper at just that period if they had had it. The first attempts at paper-making resulted in a crude, coarse product that was regarded with great scorn by the rich; and as for printed matter, the educated classes considered it a great drop from handwork and too common a thing to be purchased."

"How ridiculous!"

"It smacked of the masses," laughed Mr. Cameron. "Elegant persons refused to use anything so cheap. Snobbery existed among the ancients, you see, quite as extensively as in our own day, and a possession was only valuable while it was the property of the fortunate few. The instant it came within the reach of everybody it was no longer desirable in their eyes. Your snob always treasures a thing less for its intrinsic value than because other people cannot have it. So it was among the snobs that lived hundreds of years ago; the species has not materially changed. No sooner did learning become general through the use of the printing press, and become accessible to the man in moderate circumstances than it lost its savor for the rich, and many a noble boasted that he was unable to read, write, or spell. Learning suddenly became a vulgar accomplishment, a thing to be spurned, ridiculed, and avoided."

"I never heard of anything so absurd!" Paul said with contempt.

"It is no more absurd than is much of our present-day phi-losophy of life," replied Mr. Cameron. "With all our enlighten-ment we have not yet outgrown many of our follies."

He stopped, smiling whimsically to himself.

Paul bent over the richly colored pages on the table.

"I don't see," he remarked, "how they ever bound such stuff as this."

"The books of that early time were indeed a marvel," mused

his father. "They were not at all like the books we know now. Most of them were ponderous affairs with board covers from one to two inches thick. Around many of these covers went a metal band, usually of iron, to keep the boards from warping; and in addition this band was frequently fastened across the front with a mammoth clasp. Sometimes there were even two of these bands. The corners also were protected with metal, and to guard the great volume from wear while it lay upon its side, massive, round-headed nails studded both covers. More of these big nails were set in the metal corners."

"The thing must have weighed a ton!" exclaimed Paul.

"A single book was a far heavier commodity than you would have cared to hold in your lap," smiled Mr. Cameron. "In fact, it was impossible to hold one of them; hence we find the old-time reading desk used as a support. It was indispensable."

"But what on earth could a person do with such a book?" asked Paul. "Two or three of them would fill a room."

"Almost," laughed his father. "People did not pretend to own many of them. In the first place they cost too much; and in the next place one could not have them lying about because the nails in their sides scratched the tables. Nor could they be arranged side by side on a shelf, as we arrange books now, because of the projecting nails or buttons. Their weight, too, was a menace to safety. Petrarch almost lost his leg by having a volume of Cicero which he was reading fall on it."

"I always thought Cicero would much better be left alone!" cut in Paul wickedly. "Thank goodness that although I have to study Latin, I don't have to do it out of a book of that size!"

"You do right to make the most of your blessings," his father answered, with a twinkle in his eye. "Such books were, to say the least, awkward to handle. Most of them were kept chained to the lecterns or desks of the churches; sometimes even to the pillars."

"Chained?"

"Yes, indeed," nodded Mr. Cameron. "Books were too precious and rare to risk their being stolen, as they doubtless would have been had they been left about."

"I shouldn't think anybody would have wanted to carry a book big as the dictionary very far."

"But suppose you were very eager to learn to read and never had the chance to lay hands on a book?"

"Oh, that would be different."

"That was the condition most of the persons faced who were not rich enough to purchase books, or have access to them as the scholars in the monasteries had. For at that period of history, you must recall, the Church was the custodian of learning. Priests wrote the books, copied them, had charge of such meager libraries as there were, and taught the people. There were neither schools nor libraries like ours. What wonder that the public was ignorant and illiterate?"

Paul was thoughtful for a moment or two.

"Maybe schools are not such a bad thing, Dad," he remarked, half in fun. "They are dreadfully inconvenient, to be sure, when you want to go and play football; still I guess we are better off with them than we should be without them."

"I reckon you'd think so, were you to try the experiment of being without any," replied Mr. Cameron. "By the way, how is your football team coming on? I have not heard much about it lately."

"I haven't had time to go out with the fellows for any practice work," confessed Paul, "so I am not so well up in what they are doing as I ought to be. This paper of ours keeps me hopping. We want to make the first issue a bully one—so good that everybody who hasn't subscribed will want to, double-quick. The girls are working up a fine department on Red Cross, canning, and all that sort of thing. I've allowed them three pages for articles and items. Hazel Clement is at the head of it. She's a corking girl, and her mother is going to help her some. Mrs. Clement has been on all sorts of planning boards and committees, and National Leagues and things," concluded Paul vaguely.

"It would be interesting to get Mrs. Clement to write you an article some time," suggested Mr. Cameron.

"Do you suppose she would?"

"Certainly. She is a very public-spirited woman; moreover, she is quite as much interested in the boys and girls of Burmingham as the rest of us are, I am sure."

"I've a great mind to ask her," said Paul. "If we could get one fine article a month from some parent who has something to say, it would help us tremendously. Of course, it would have to be on something the scholars would be keen on though: home gardens, or earning money, or citizenship, or making things."

"I am certain that if you explained your editorial policy to some of the grown-ups they would submit manuscripts to you," returned Mr. Cameron mischievously. "You would not be obliged to bind yourself to publish them if they were not satisfactory. Editors are always at liberty to send contributions back with a slip saying that the inclosed article does not meet the needs of their paper, or else that there is no room for it."

"Gee! Imagine my sending back an article that some parent had written."

"If you are going to be an editor that will be part of your business. You will have to learn to discriminate between the articles that are timely, well written, interesting, and in harmony with the principles you have blocked out for your magazine."

"Do you suppose Mr. Carter has to do that?" asked Paul in an awed tone.

"Without question."

"Then no wonder he looks as if he would freeze the blood in your veins," ejaculated the boy. "It must make him almighty severe just to keep reading stuff and sending back what he doesn't like, regardless of who wrote it."

"He must keep up the standard of his paper, son. His subscribers pay good money for it and they want what they pay for. Were an editor to take pity on every poor soul who sent him an article his publication would soon be filled with every sort of trash. He has to train himself to be unprejudiced and give his readers only the best the market affords. The personal element does not enter into the matter."

"I see. I hadn't thought of that side of it," Paul confessed slowly.

His father watched him in silence.

"I should not let this matter worry me," observed the older man presently, "for I doubt if you have so many unsolicited manuscripts that you will be troubled with returning a great number of them to their owners. And if you find yourself overrun with them you can always call in expert advice."

Paul brightened.

"I could ask somebody's opinion, couldn't I?" he declared.

"Of course. Or you could consult with your staff."

"My staff! Pooh! They wouldn't know any more about it than I did," chuckled Paul. "But you would, Dad, and so would Judge Damon. I shall come straight to you if I get stuck."

"Two heads are often better than one," responded Mr. Cameron kindly. "Bring your problem home, my boy, if you find it too big for you. Together we'll thrash it out."

"You certainly are a trump, Dad!" cried Paul. "I guess between us all we can make a go of the *March Hare*."

"I'm sure of it!" responded his father.

CHAPTER VI

A GAME OF CARDS

The first copy of the *March Hare* came out amid great excitement,—excitement that spread not only through the Burmingham High School but into the home of almost every child in the town. It was a good number, exceptionally so, even as the product of an undergraduate body of students who were most of them amateurs at the writing game.

A page of the magazine was given up to each of the classes and contained items of interest to freshmen, sophomores, juniors, and seniors respectively; there was a page of alumnæ notes; another page devoted to general school news; a section on school sports; another section on girls' clubs and handicraft. The drawing master contributed a page or two on poster-making; and Mrs. Clement was prevailed upon to write a bright and practical article on the making of an iceless refrigerator.

Even Mr. Carter, old newspaper warhorse that he was, was compelled to admit that the *March Hare* was not half so mad as it was painted. In fact, he grudgingly owned to one of his employees that the new publication was quite a masterpiece for the youngsters. He had not dreamed they could do so well. It was a great surprise to him. Why, the product was quite an eye opener! A paper for general home use might not be such a bad thing in Burmingham. There was actually something in this *March Hare* worth while for grown-ups. If the following issues continued to be of the present order of merit, the *Echo* had nothing to blush for in fostering the scheme. As for that Paul Cameron, he was a boy worth watching. He would make his mark some day.

Coming from a man who habitually said so little, such praise was phenomenal and it spurred Paul, to whom it was repeated, to increased effort. He must keep his paper up to this standard, that was certain.

With such a varied group of opinions to harmonize as was represented by his editorial staff, this was not altogether an easy task. Each boy stressed the thing he was specially interested in and saw no reason for publishing anything else in the paper. Some thought more room should be given to athletics; some clamored that the "highbrow stuff" be cut out; others were for choking off the girls' articles on canning and fancy work. There were hectic meetings at which the youthful literary pioneers squabbled, and debated, and almost came to blows.

But Paul Cameron was a boy of unusual tact. He heard each objector in turn and patiently smoothed away his objections until, upon a battlefield of argument from which scars of bitterness might have survived, a harmonious body of workers finally stood shoulder to shoulder, each with enthusiasm to make the particular part of the work for which he was responsible finer and more efficient. It was, as Paul declared to his colleagues, a triumph of teamwork.

It had never, perhaps, come to the minds of the boys that teamwork was a term that could be applied to work as well as to play. Business and sport seemed vitally different fields of activity. Yet here they were—a group of boys pulling together, each at the post assigned him—toiling for the success of the whole body.

Was it such a different thing from football or baseball after all? Business managers, authors, advertising agents, were working quite as hard to do their part as ever they had worked at right or left tackle; as first baseman, or pitcher, or catcher. The present task simply demanded a different type of energy, that was all. The same old slogan of each for the whole was applicable.

Consequently every man took up his duties with a pride in his especial role on the team, and as a result the second issue of the *March Hare* over-topped the first, and the third the second.

Young people who did not go to the High School at all mailed subscriptions to the business manager; the alumnæ, now scattered in every direction, began to write for the publication to be sent them; it was good, they said, to get once more into touch with their Alma Mater. Older persons who had no children turned in applications for the *March Hare*. They had seen a copy of the paper and liked it.

Into Paul's editorial sanctum articles from parents who had things to say and wished to say them gradually found their way. Many of these persons had done little writing and would not have presumed to send their attempts to a magazine of a more professional character.

Mr. Lemuel Hardy, for example, submitted a humorous poem on how the grapes disappeared from his stone wall,—a poem so amusing and so good-natured yet withal containing such a pitiful little refrain of disappointment that the seniors at once took it upon themselves to see that no more of Lemuel's grapes were molested.

Mrs. Wilbur wrote on raising, transplanting, and caring for currant bushes. Was it really so hard as that to bring a good crop of fruit to perfection? If so, the boy was a brute who invaded Mrs. Wilbur's garden. 1920 would see that there was no more of that!

Gladys Marvin's father sent to the paper a short article on the beauty of the ordinary stones when polished and offered to polish, for a small sum, any specimen brought him. Many of the pupils of the school availed themselves of this suggestion, and before a month was out there blossomed forth a host of stones of every imaginable hue set in rings or scarfpins of silver. Stone-hunting became a craze and the geological department gained scores of pupils in consequence. One heard murmurs about quartz and crystals as one passed through the school corridors, and one came upon eager scientists comparing rings, brooches, or pendants.

The drawing department was beset with pupils who wished either to make designs for jewelry, or to look over books on ancient settings for gems.

Louise Clausen had a necklace she had made herself at arts and crafts class; it was set with stones she had collected—common pebbles that had been polished—and it was the envy of the entire student body. Her mother had let her melt up an old silver butter-dish to make it, she explained.

Burmingham boys and girls went home *en masse* and begged to be allowed to melt up old water pitchers, mugs, or napkin rings, and fashion jewelry.

Out of the jumble of material turned in from various sources one number after another of the *March Hare* appeared, each marked by a freshness of subject matter and a freedom of expression in such complete contrast to other publications that even such an august medium as the *Echo* broke over its traditions to a sufficient extent to glean an idea here and there from the infant prodigy and enlarge upon it.

Once no less a personage than Mr. Arthur Presby Carter himself asked of Paul permission to reprint in the columns of his paper an article that had particularly appealed to him as unique and interesting.

"I tried," declared Paul, when relating the incident to his father, "not to fall all over myself when granting the permission. I told him that of course the thing was copyrighted, but that we should be glad to have him use it on the condition that he printed the source from which he had obtained it. One of his men told me afterward that we let him off too easy—that Carter was determined to have the article, and would have paid us a good sum for the privilege of republishing it. We never thought of charging him for it; we were proud as Punch to have him reprint it."

Mr. Cameron laughed. Paul's frankness had always been one of the lad's greatest charms.

"Pride goeth before destruction, my son," he remarked jestingly. "However, perhaps you did as well not to put a price on your product. Mr. Carter has done quite a little to boost your undertaking and you can afford to grant him a favor or two. But I will say you are getting pretty deep into newspaper work, Paul."

"I do seem to be, don't I?" smiled Paul, flushing boyishly. "I'm crazy over it, too. The more you do at it the better you like it. I don't know but that when I'm through college, I'd like to go in and be a reporter. I'd like to write up fires and accidents and wear a little badge that would admit me inside the lines at parades and political meetings."

"I'm afraid you'd find there was lots to it besides the badge and the pleasure of stalking under the ropes."

"I suppose so; but I'd like the chance to try it. I've always envied those chaps who whispered some magic word and walked in while the rest of us waited outside."

"There you go!" cried his father. "You are just as bad at

wanting what other people cannot have as ever were the early book collectors!"

Paul colored.

"I know it," he admitted. "I'm afraid we all enjoy having a pull and getting the best of other people. It is human nature."

"It is human, that is true; nevertheless, the impulse is a very selfish one," said his father.

A silence fell upon the two. They were sitting in the living room and it was almost Paul's bedtime. Outside the rain was beating on the windows; but inside a fire crackled on the hearth and a crimson glow from the silken lampshade made cheery the room.

"I was telling the fellows to-day some of the things you told me about early bookmaking, Dad," remarked Paul. "They wanted to know if printing came soon after the illuminated books, and who invented it. I couldn't answer their question and as yet have had no time to look up the matter. We had quite a discussion about it. Perhaps you can save me the trouble of overhauling an encyclopedia."

"I've no business to save you from such an expedition," retorted Mr. Cameron with amusement. "Morally, the best thing you can do is to look up the answer to your question yourself. It is good for you. However, because the subject happens to interest me, I am going to be weak enough to reply to your query. Printing did follow the hand-illuminated and hand-penned manuscripts and books; but before printed books made their appearance, there was an interval when printers tried to say what they had to say by means of pictures. You know how we give a child a picture book as a first approach to more serious reading. He is too undeveloped to comprehend printed words; but he can understand pictures. It was just so in the olden days.

The uneducated masses of people were as simple as children. Hence the pioneer printers' initial efforts were turned in the direction of playing cards, pictures for home decoration—or *images*, as they were called—and genuine picture books, where the entire story was told by a series of illustrations."

Mr. Cameron paused in his narrative.

"You can readily see, if you think for a moment," he presently went on, "how such an innovation came about. Paper had not been invented, and vellum was not only costly but too limited in supply to permit many books being printed. Moreover, as I told you, hand in hand with this objection was the fact that the majority of the public had no interest in learning. Their intellects were immature. They were nothing but grown-up children, and you know how children like games and picture books. Well, those are the reasons why the next step in the development of printing was in the direction of making playing cards. A coarse, thick, yellowish paper was beginning to be produced—the first crude attempt at paper-making—and on this material were engraved woodcuts of varying degrees of artistic merit. Some of the designs were merely ugly and clumsy; but some, on the other hand, were really exquisite examples of hand-coloring, unique and quaint in pattern. Thus playing cards came speedily into vogue. The finest ones were painted on tablets of ivory, or engraved on thin sheets of silver. It is interesting, too, to note that the old conventional designs then in use have, with very little modification, persisted up to the present day. Probably the playing cards in common use were printed by the same crude method as were the images, and unfortunately history has failed to unravel just what that method was. They may possibly have been stenciled. All we have been able to learn is that cards, images (which were in reality religious pictures), and stenciled altar cloths—the first primitive printing on cloth—all appeared very early in southern Europe, playing cards having their origin in Venice, where in 1400 and even before that date we read of the Venetians playing cards."

"Do you suppose their games were anything like ours?" questioned Paul, much interested.

"I doubt it. Probably, for example, there was no bridge whist in those days," said his father, with a chuckle. "And I'll wager, too, the Venetians were quite as happy and as well off without it. The games of the time were doubtless much more simple. But whatever they were, they proved to be so fascinating that they soon became an actual menace. Amusements were few in those dull, monotonous days, when there were neither theaters, books, moving pictures, railroads, or automobiles. One day was much like another. Therefore even the clergy welcomed a diversion and devoted so much time to cards that the recreation had to be forbidden them. Now and then some great religious movement would sweep over the land and break up card-playing; but after a little respite people always returned to it with even greater zest than before. Nor was it a wholly bad thing. In the absence of schools the games quickened the intellect and made the common people mentally more alert; the ignorant were also trained by this means to count and solve simple problems in arithmetic, of which most of them knew nothing."

"That's a funny way to get arithmetic lessons," said Paul.

"Yet you can see that a knowledge of numbers could be thus obtained?"

"Why, yes. Of course. But I never thought of it before."

"Remember that the race had reverted to its childhood during the Dark Ages," explained Mr. Cameron. "For years all its attention had been given to warfare, and learning and the arts which had been destroyed by constant strife and turmoil had to be built up again."

"But to have people learn arithmetic by means of playing cards!" mused Paul.

"Better that way than not at all. It helped the big result by gradually making them realize how little they knew, and making them want to know more, which was the necessary spur to learning. You will be interested also to know, since we are discussing playing cards, that the four suits are said to represent the four great social classes of society at that time. Hearts stood for the clergy; Spades (spada meaning a sword) for the nobility; Clubs for the peasantry; and Diamonds for the more prosperous citizens or burghers."

"That is interesting, isn't it?"

"Yes, I think so."

"And the images?"

"Oh, the image-prints were small religious pictures done in color," answered his father, "and I fear they were often valued far more for their brilliant hues than for their religious significance. They represented all sorts of subjects, being taken largely from incidents in the lives of the saints. You know that at that time in many countries, especially in Italy, religious dramas were presented—plays such as Everyman and Saint George and the Dragon. Hence such scenes were constantly before the people, and they were very familiar with them. The small image-prints served to perpetuate to a great extent things which they liked and knew; and the picture books, which gave not only these scenes in other form, but also reproduced stories from the Bible, did the same. No text was necessary. The picture told the tale to a people who could not read, just as the stained-glass windows and mosaics in the churches did. Everywhere the feeble literature of the period took the form either of verbal minstrelsy, drama, or pictured representations. You will recall how most of the early races first wrote in pictures instead of letters. There were hieroglyphics in Egypt; 'speaking stories' in Assyria; and picture-writing in Turkey, China, and Japan. The picture book of the time was merely an attempt to put into simple outline, by means of woodcuts, the religious drama, or dumb shows of the day. The city of Florence did much for this form of work, its *rappresentazioni* being printed as early as 1485. Albrecht Dürer of Germany was one of the later and most skilful woodcut artists. What the ballad was to literature the woodcut was to art—simple, direct, appealing."

The man paused.

"The printed story awaited several necessary factors to bring it into being. One was a public that desired to read—which this one did not; another was a means by which to print reading matter; a third was suitable paper on which to print; and the fourth, but by no means the least important, a good and proper quality of ink. One after another these difficulties were done away with. If they had not been," concluded Mr. Cameron, "you would not now have been publishing such a thing as the *March Hare*."

CHAPTER VII

A MAD TEA PARTY

It was amazing to see how the general interest in the *March Hare* increased as the months went by. So successful was the magazine that Paul ventured an improvement in the way of a patriotic cover done in three colors—an eagle and an American flag designed by one of the juniors and submitted for acceptance in a "cover contest", the prize offered being a year's subscription to the paper. After this innovation came the yet more pretentious and far-reaching novelty of the Mad Tea Party, a supper held in the hall of the school with seventy-five-cent tickets for admission. The mothers of the pupils contributed the food, and as Burmingham boasted many an expert cook the meal spread upon the tables was indeed a royal one.

The edict went forth that no guest would be admitted to the festival unless arrayed in an "Alice in Wonderland" costume, and for the sake of witnessing the fun, as well as of helping forward the fête, more than one dignified resident of the town struggled into an incongruous garment and mingled in the train of Alice, the White Queen, the Red Queen, the Duchess, Father William, and the Aged Man. Judge Damon and Mr. Cameron provoked a storm of mirth by appearing as the Walrus and the Carpenter, and Paul's mother, who was still a young and pretty woman, came as the famous Queen of Hearts. As for Mr. Carter, although

More Than One Dignified Resident Of The Town
Struggled Into An Incongruous Garment.

he pooh-poohed the idea and made all manner of jokes about the party, he astonished the entire community by presenting himself at the last moment as the Dormouse.

Such a revel had not taken place in the village for years. In fact, there had never before been any social function which brought high and low, rich and poor together in such democratic fashion. The frolic had in it a Mardi Gras spirit quite foreign to the wonted quiet and dignity of the place.

"Why, we haven't had such a shaking-up in years!" ejaculated the postmaster. "Seems like we've all got better acquainted with our neighbors in this one evening than we ever did in all the rest of our lives put together. You don't get far at knowing a man if you just bow to him every day; but when you go making an ape of yourself and he goes making an ape of himself, each of you finds out how human the other one is. You've got something in common to talk about."

And it was even as the old postmaster declared. Many a social barrier was broken down and forgotten as a result of the *March Hare* carnival. Parents ceased to remember their differences by talking together about their children, a topic that never failed to bring them into sympathy. Thus the movement which had its source in an impulse to aid the youngsters proved to be of benefit also to many of the elders. Nor was this the only consequence of the event.

Into the coffers of the class treasury poured undreamed-of wealth which made possible the gift of two fine pictures to the school,—one of Washington and one of Lincoln; a large cast of the Winged Victory was purchased as well, and placed in an empty niche in the assembly hall. Thus did 1920 leave behind it a memory illustrious and not to be forgotten.

In the meantime Paul, absorbed in this successful undertaking, was so busy that he had scarcely leisure to eat. The editing of the paper demanded more and more time, and as new problems were constantly arising concerning its publication he did not neglect to glean from every possible direction all the information he could about printing. The mere act of preparing copy for the press opened to his alert mind a multitude of inquiries.

"I read to-day," he announced to his father one evening, "that the printing press was invented by Lawrence Coster (or Lorenz Koster) of Haarlem. The book said that he went on a picnic with his family, and while idly carving his name on the trunk of a beech tree he conceived the idea that he might in the same way make individual letters of the alphabet on wooden blocks, ink them over, and thus print words."

Mr. Cameron listened attentively.

"Such is the old legend," he replied. "It is an interesting one and many persons believe it to this day. History, however, fails to bear out the tale. Instead, as nearly as we can find out, what Coster is really conceded to have done was not to invent printing but to be the first to make movable type, which was one of the greatest factors in the perfecting of the industry. Holland has done honor, and rightly, to the inventor by placing a statue of him at Haarlem; but the real inventor of printing was probably John Gutenburg, a native of Strasbourg, who made a printing press which, although not so elaborate as that in present use, was nevertheless a properly constructed one. Simple as it was, the principle of it is identical with that used to-day."

"That is curious, isn't it?" observed Paul.

"Yes. Think how long ago it was; from 1440 to 1460 he toiled at his invention. He was a versatile man, being not only skilled in polishing precious stones but also at making mirrors. The making of mirrors was a new trade in Germany for outside the borders of Venice, where the monopoly had long been held by Italian workmen, the industry was almost unknown. It is possible that Gutenburg may have used the presses and even the lead employed for molding the mirror frames to work out his metal type. Doubtless his knowledge of melting and pouring lead was derived from his mirror-making trade. We know, however, little of his experiments. He worked in secret, spending years in research and wasting other years in delays, when money to further his invention was not forthcoming. His first printing was done about 1439 or 1440, and from that time up to 1460 he was busy printing and struggling to make his work more perfect."

"What did he print in those early days?" inquired Paul. "Books?"

"Yes. A few pages from them remain and are to be seen at the National Library at Paris. The letters used are very coarse and uneven and are in the Latin type employed by the monks in writing their manuscripts. It is almost a romance to picture Gutenburg shut up in the old ruined monastery where he worked night and day with one of his faithful helpers—a goldsmith who had long been in his employ—and two other tried and trusty apprentices. You can see how necessary it was that he have men whom he could rely on not to divulge his secret. Probably the goldsmith's knowledge of metals was of service to his master in the undertaking; as for the joiner who had previously aided in constructing mirror frames, he made most of the tools. We don't know much about the third workman, but we do know that later one of the trio died very suddenly, and the interruption to Gutenburg's work caused great delay. Fearful that in the meantime the secret of the invention might leak out, or that the old servant's heirs might insist on having a share in the discovery,

Gutenburg melted up his forms and abandoned further labor for a time. This was a great pity, for by destroying what he had done the inventor had it all to create over again later on. His rash act did, however, prove one thing which history wanted to know, and that was that Gutenburg used metal forms and not wood to make his letters."

"How soon did he re-make his metal forms?" asked Paul eagerly.

"Not right away," responded Mr. Cameron. "He was deeply in debt and a good deal discouraged by the death of his efficient workman on whom he was very dependent. For six years we hear no more of him. Then he appeared at Metz where he began borrowing money again, just as he had done before. He was fortunate in securing the aid needed, and it is from this period on that his best printing was done. He now branched out into more ambitious tasks, producing a copy of the Latin Bible in three volumes. This pretentious undertaking of course required a great many letters, and he found that to cut them by hand was too slow a process; moreover, the lead letters were very soft and wore down quickly. He must cast his letters in brass molds and make them of more durable metal. But alas, such an innovation was costly and his money had given out. Therefore, much as he dreaded to part with his secret, he was forced to take into partnership a rich metal worker by the name of John Faust."

Mr. Cameron paused to think a moment.

"It was thus that Gutenburg procured the brass for his molds; made in them letters of harder material; and printed his Bible. With the production of this masterpiece came a strange happening, too. You can see that by printing from letters cast in molds the text was more regular than was the handwork done by the priests and monks. Hence when Charles VII of France saw one of the new Bibles he was enchanted with it and eagerly bought it because of its uniform text. The next day he displayed his recently acquired treasure to the Archbishop with no little pride, and great was his astonishment when the Archbishop asserted with promptness that he himself owned a newly purchased Bible that was quite as perfect in execution. The king protested that such a miracle could not be—that no one could write by hand two such copies. To settle the dispute the Archbishop's Bible was produced and placed beside the king's, and there they were, identically the same. The dignitaries were troubled. It was not humanly possible to pen by hand two such books. Why, it would take a lifetime—more than a lifetime; nor could any penman write two manuscripts so exactly alike. To make the matter worse and more puzzling, other copies were discovered precisely like the king's and the Archbishop's. Not a line or letter varied. It was magic!"

Paul laughed with pleasure.

"No wonder the poor king and the stately archbishop were upset!" he said.

"They were very much upset indeed," agreed his father. "It was, you must recall, a superstitious age. Everything that could not be fathomed was attributed to witchcraft. Hence witchcraft was the only explanation of the present miracle. John Faust, of whom the two royal persons had bought the books, must have sold himself to the devil. They would have the unlucky merchant brought, and if he could not satisfactorily tell how and where he had got the Bibles, he should be burned alive."

"I suppose he went and told!" put in Paul indignantly.

"Yes, he did. He wasn't going to forfeit his life. I fancy any of us would have done the same, too. He showed the Archbishop his press and explained how the Bibles had been printed."

"It was a pity he had to."

"It was something of a pity," answered Mr. Cameron. "And yet the secret must have come out sometime, I suppose, for subsequently Faust quarreled with Gutenburg and by and by set up a press of his own at Metz, and with two printing presses in the same town, and the workmen necessary to run them mingling with the populace, it was impossible to keep such an invention from the public. Gradually it became common property and it had become universal when Metz was sacked in the Franco-Prussian War, its printing rooms destroyed, and the workmen scattered."

"Did that put an end to printing?" questioned Paul.

"No. On the contrary it spread the art over France and Germany. By 1500 there were over fifty presses on the continent. In the meantime William Caxton, an English merchant, traveled to Holland to buy cloth, and there became so much interested in the books he saw and the tale of how they were printed that he purchased some type and, bringing it home, set up a printing press in London not far from Westminster Abbey. The first English book to be printed was dated 1474 and was called 'The Game of Chess.' Then came a Bible which was presented to the king. From this time on there was practically an end to the handwritten books made by the monks in cloisters and monasteries. Occasionally such a volume was made for the very rich because, as I told you, the elegant still considered paper and the printed book too common and cheap for their use. But with the steady improvement of ink and paper and the awakening desire of the masses to read what was printed came the dawn of religious liberty and the birth of learning."

"It is a wonderful story!" cried Paul, much moved.

"A book in itself, isn't it?" said his father. "It is an interesting fact, however, that Latin and the Latin text continued to be the language of the printed book for some time; this was not only because of an established precedent, but because the Renaissance in Italy revived an interest in classic literature. But by and by people demanded books in their native tongue. They wished to read something besides the classics—literature that was alive and a part of their own era. The written *novello*, or story, began to take the place of the ballads which the *trouveurs*, or minstrels who wandered from castle to castle, had chanted. One was no longer dependent on such a story-teller. The printed novel had arrived. Its form was still very crude, but it was nevertheless a story and a broader field for entertainment than was provided by the threadbare lives of the saints. Science, too, was making remarkable progress and the public was alert to read of Bacon and Galileo, as well as of Luther and Shakespeare. Had printing come earlier it would have been to a passive, indifferent populace; now it appeared in answer to the craving of a people thirsty to read of travel, invention, poetry; to consume the Tales of King Arthur, Sir John Mandeville's Travels, Sidney's 'Arcadia', Chaucer's Canterbury Tales. The Elizabethans reflected in England the rebirth of literature and learning which was sweeping all Europe at the time. Printing was not the herald, nor yet the servant, of this wonderful age; but was rather its companion, going hand in hand with it and making all the wealth of thought that it had to give available to us, as well as to those of its own day."

"Long live Gutenburg!" exclaimed Paul.

"Yes, we owe him a great deal," agreed Mr. Cameron. "But do not become confused and attribute everything to him. He did invent type molds for casting type and thereby brought printing to the point of a practical art. He did not invent engraving on wood, as many enthusiasts acclaim; nor did he invent impressions of relief surfaces. He was not, moreover, the first to print on paper, for the makers of playing cards and image-prints had done that before him. There had also been roughly printed books before his day and printing presses, too. There had even been movable type. But Gutenburg was the first to combine these ideas so that they could be used for practical purposes. In other words, he was the first practical typographer, not the first printer. Upon the foundation that other men had built in, he reared a permanent, useful art without which there could not have been either enlightenment or education."

CHAPTER VIII

THE ROMANCE OF BOOKMAKING

Ever since last night, Dad," remarked Paul, the next evening at dinner, "I have been wondering how the old printers got rid of the Latin text, lettering, or whatever you call it, and got down to printing in English like ours."

"You're starting on a long story," replied Mr. Cameron, glancing up from his plate. "The development of our modern type requires a volume in itself. Many scholars and many craftsmen contributed to that glorious result. It did not come all in a minute. Gutenburg's uneven Latin lettering was a far cry from our uniform, clear, well-designed variety of print. In the first place, as I told you before, good ink and good paper were necessary to beautiful text, and these Gutenburg did not have. Gradually, however, as a result of repeated experiments, paper and ink that were of practical value were manufactured. China had long been successful in printing because of the fine texture of her paper. Italy, the home of the arts, caught up Gutenburg's invention and brought not only lettering but paper-making to a marvelous degree of perfection."

"Italy and China always seem to be doing things," laughed Paul.

"Both nations were inventive and original," answered Mr.

Cameron. "The difference between them was that while China locked all her discoveries up within her own walled cities, Italy shared her knowledge with the rest of the world and made it and herself immortal."

"The Italians were a great people, weren't they?"

"They were true lovers of all that was best and most beautiful," answered his father gravely. "Even their aristocracy felt it no disgrace to toil to perfect a fine art. To make that which was excellent more excellent still was the aim of rich and poor. Nobles, artisans, barefooted friars worked together towards that common goal. It was an Italian prince, Nicholas V, a man who afterward became Pope, who founded the Vatican Library and collected five thousand books, at a time, you must remember, when a book was a rare and almost priceless treasure. To him we owe the preservation of many a valuable old manuscript that might otherwise have been destroyed. Five thousand volumes was in those days a vast number to get together."

"Our public libraries would not think so now," smiled Paul.

"No, because at present books are so easily within reach that we scarcely appreciate them. We certainly read only a very small proportion of them."

"I know I don't read many," said Paul soberly.

"You will read more as you grow older, son," returned his father kindly. "But most of us are intellectually lazy; even grown-up persons devote a good part of their short lives to reading things that profit them nothing."

"Things like the *March Hare*, for example," suggested Paul facetiously.

"Many a worse thing than the *March Hare*, I'm afraid," his father responded. "We seem to think we have unlimited time before us, and that there is no hurry about reading the good things we mean to read before we die; so we waste our precious moments on every sort of trash—cheap novels, worthless magazines, newspaper gossip, and before we know it, our lives are gone. I overlook your being so foolish; but for me it is inexcusable. The Italians of the Renaissance did not give themselves over to such folly. They put their hearts seriously into building up their age and generation. Lorenzo de Medici dragged from the corners of Europe and Asia some two hundred Greek and Latin manuscripts. Other Florentines, Venetians, Romans collected private libraries. Princes of the land turned their wealth not to their own idle pleasure but to financing Gutenburg's invention and establishing printing presses which the culture and brain of the country controlled. There was a printing press at the Vatican itself, and scholars who were paid large salaries met in consultation concerning the literature printed. The best artists contributed their skill to the undertaking. Indeed, it was a disagreement about some theological work that Martin Luther had come from Germany to help with that sent him back home in a temper. And not only was the matter printed carefully scrutinized but also every detail of its production was thought out—the size of the page, the size of the type, the width of the margins, the quality of the paper, the variety of type to be used. What wonder that under such conditions printing was rapidly transformed from a trade to an art. When we think of the exquisite books made in this far-away day, we sigh at our present output."

Mr. Cameron's face clouded, then brightened.

"Nevertheless when all is said and done, books are not for the person of wealth alone. The work of the Aldi of Italy, the Elzevirs of Leyden, the Estiennes of Paris, although of finest quality, was much too expensive for universal use. For it is the subject matter inside the book which, when all is said and done, is the thing we are after, and which we are eager to spread abroad; and never in any age has every type of literature been so cheap and accessible, or the average of culture so high as now. If a person is ignorant to-day it is his own fault. Nothing stands between him and the stars but his own laziness and indifference."

"*Time*, my dear Henry," interrupted Mrs. Cameron. "Do not leave out the element of time. Remember that the farther away we get from the beginning of learning, the greater accumulation there is for us to master. Like a mammoth snowball, each century has rolled up its treasure until such a mass has come down to us that it is practically impossible for us to possess ourselves of it. Sometimes when I think of all there is to know, I am depressed."

"And me, too, Mater," echoed Paul. "It seems hopeless."

"But there are short outs," argued Mr. Cameron. "No one expects any of us to read all the books of the past. The years have sifted the wheat from the chaff, and by a process of elimination we have found out pretty well by this time what the great books are. By classifying our subjects we can easily trace the growth and development of any of the really significant movements of the world; we can follow the path of the sciences; study the progress of the drama from its infancy to the present moment; trace the growth of the novel; note the perfecting of the poetic form. History, philosophy, the thought of all the ages is ours. That is what I mean when I say there is no excuse for persons of our era being uninformed. We are reaping the results of many unfoldings and can see things with a degree of completeness that our ancestors could not; they looked at life's problems from the bottom of the hill and got only a partial view; we are seeing them from the top, and understanding—or we should be understanding—more fully, their interrelation."

"I suppose," mused Paul thoughtfully, "that those who come after us will see even farther than we."

"They ought to, and I believe they will," his father answered. "*Nothing walks with aimless feet*, in my opinion. It is all part of a gigantic, divine plan. The small beginnings of the past have been the seed of to-day's harvest. We thank Gutenburg for our books. We thank such men as Nicholas V and many another of his ilk for the Vatican Library, the British Museum, the numberless foreign museums; we owe a debt to our nation for our own Congressional Library, to say nothing of the smaller ones that, through the public spirit of generous citizens, have opened their doors to our people and done so much to educate and democratize our country."

There was a moment of silence.

"And quite aside from the thousands of volumes written in our own language, we have access to the literature of other nations both in translation and in their mother tongue. Remember that after printing had got well under way, type in other languages—Arabic, Greek, Hebrew—had to be developed in order that the literature of other languages might augment our own."

"I don't think I took that into account," remarked Paul.

"Of course," continued Mr. Cameron less seriously, "not every person of the olden time was alert for learning. Human nature was much the same then as now.

"I'm afraid even in the midst of all this thirst for knowledge there were those who cared far more for the outside of a book than for the inside," he continued humorously. "Books were bound in brocade, in richly ornamented leather embossed with gilt; some had covers of gold or silver studded with gems, while others were adorned with carved ivory or enamel. As time went on and the religious manuscripts written, illuminated, and bound by the monks gave place to the more elaborate productions of a printing age, ecclesiasts were not skilful enough to do the illustrating demanded, and a guild of bookbinders sprang up. Into the hands of artists outside the cloister were put the more dainty and worldly pictures required by secular text. Then followed a period when scholars who owned books were no longer forced to loan them to students to copy for their own use, as had been the case in the past. Books became less expensive and were accessible to everybody. Slowly they were got into more practical form—were made smaller and less bulky; not only outside but inside they were improved. 'The Lives of Saints' and Fox's 'Book of Martyrs' gave way first to the tales of Merlin and King Arthur in various versions, stories of Charlemagne, and romances of similar character. Copyrights being unknown, there was no law to protect a book, and hence all the adventures of the hero of any one tongue were passed on to the favorite hero of another nationality; as a result French, Italian, Spanish, and Celtic literature teem with heroes who perform marvellous deeds of identical character."

Paul was amused.

"Amadis of France, the popular idol of the French people, worked the same marvels as King Arthur did, only under another name. Every nation borrowed (or rather stole) from every other. It was not considered reprehensible to do so. Shakespeare worked over the Italian *novelle* of Boccaccio, weaving them into his great English dramas, and nobody censured him. It was this craving for romance that overcame the delight in mere display and roused interest not alone in the binding of a book but in its contents. True collectors and book-fanciers still strove with one another to obtain choice, beautiful, and fabulously expensive volumes. But for the most part the book came back to its original purpose and took its place as a mouthpiece of literature."

"Do you mean that books became cheap?" asked Paul.

"Not what we should consider cheap—that is, not for a long time. You see, the thing that makes a book cheap is not alone the material put into it, or the price for which it can be obtained of the author; it is largely the size of the edition printed that reduces the expense of production. It is practically as much work to print fifty copies of a volume as several hundred. The labor of setting the type is the same. The circle of readers was not large enough in olden times to justify a volume being manufactured in large numbers; nor were there any methods for advertising and distributing books broadcast as there are now."

"Oh," exclaimed Paul, "I see. Of course there weren't."

"Advertising and distribution play a very important part in our present-day book trade," his father went on. "To-day publishers frequently announce and advertise the book of a well-known author before the manuscript is completed, sometimes even before it is written at all. They get a scenario or résumé of the story, and take orders for the book as if it were really already finished. Or with the manuscript in their hands they will often begin 'traveling it' long before it is printed. The reason for this is that in a large country like ours it takes a long time for salesmen to get about and secure orders from the various selling houses of our large cities. It means spreading a book from coast to coast. While the publisher is getting the book through the press, correcting proof, having illustrations and the colored jacket designed and printed, perhaps having posters made for advertising, his salesmen are taking orders for it by means of a condensation of the story and a dummy cover similar to the one which later will be put on the volume. Then, when the books are ready, they are shipped east and west, north and south, but are not released for sale until a given date, when all the stores begin selling them simultaneously. You can see that this is the only fair method, for it would be impossible, for example, for San Francisco to advertise a book as new, if it had been already selling in Boston for a month or so. All the selling houses must have the same chance. So a date of publication is usually set and announced. Frequently, however, long before that date an edition, or several editions of a popular book will be sold out. Booksellers will be so certain that they can dispose of a great number of volumes that they will place large orders ahead in order to be sure of securing the books they desire."

"Can they always tell ahead what people will want?" inquired Paul.

"No, not always. Sometimes the public will be caught by a story and it will become popular not only to the amazement of the bookseller, but to the surprise of both publisher and author as well. One cannot always prophesy what readers will like, especially if an author is new. It is a great gamble. But usually an author whose work is known and liked can safely be calculated upon to sell."

"Is it much work for a publisher to get a book ready for the market after he once gets the manuscript from the author?" asked Paul.

"To produce a well-printed, artistic book requires infinite care and pains," replied Mr. Cameron. "Of course a book can be rushed through. Such a thing is possible. But under ordinary conditions it is several months, sometimes a year, before the book is ready for sale. First a galley proof of the manuscript is made; by this I mean the subject matter is printed on a long strip of paper about the width of a page but several times as long.

Then this proof, which is made chiefly to be sure the type is correctly set, is examined, and the errors in it are rectified. After this it is again corrected and is cut up into lengths suitable for a page. Following this the page proof is printed, care being taken that the last word at the bottom of one page joins on to the top word of the next. It is very easy to omit a word and thus mar the sense. It is also a rule of most publishing houses that the top line of each page shall be a full line, and in consequence it is often a Chinese puzzle to make the text conform to the rule. Readers often have to insert a line or take one out to meet this necessity, and sometimes an author's text is garbled as a result. No writer likes having words or whole sentences introduced or omitted; and you can't quite blame him, either, for he has to stand behind the book and receive not only what praise it may win but also the blame showered on it by both the public and the reviewers. Naturally the book—not alone the story but the style and choice of words—is assumed to be his. If he is a careful worker he has probably weighed every word that has gone into the phrasing. He therefore does not relish having his style meddled with, even for such a technicality as the filling out of a short line."

"Is it really better to heed this printer's edict?" laughed Paul.

"I think without question the book makes a better appearance if the rule is heeded," declared Mr. Cameron. "A printer does and should take pride in the looks of his page. The beauty of a book is quite an element in its production. After the type has been set up and corrected, and the proof paged, the next consideration is the size of the paper to be used, the quality, the texture. The width of the margins, the clearness or brilliancy of the text, the appearance and flexibility of the binding all have to do with the artistic result which is, or should be, the aim of every publisher. When all these details have been decided upon there is yet another important factor in book-producing—the item of expense. Books being no longer the property of the few, they must be within the reach of the many, and the book-manufacturer's business is to make them so. It is precisely because we have such a large reading public that America has attained her high intellectual average. Not that we are a cultured nation. By no means. What I mean is that our public school system offers education so freely, and even compels it so drastically, that there is a much smaller proportion of illiterate persons here than in most lands. Our illiterates are largely foreigners who have not been in our country long enough to become educated. Most of them have immigrated from places where they had no educational advantages, and some of them are, alas, now too old to learn. The great part of our native-born citizens can read and write, and vast numbers of them have a much broader education than that. It is by means of the wide distribution of learning and enlightenment that we hope to banish ignorance and superstition and spread patriotism and democracy. So you see books are a giant element in our national plan, and the writing and publishing of what is worthy and helpful is a service to the country. To do all this the publisher has no easy puzzle to solve—to produce what is good literature artistically, and at a price where he shall have his legitimate profit, and yet give to the public something within the range of its purse."

"I guess I'd rather stick to my job on the *March Hare!*" exclaimed Paul.

"I imagine it is quite big enough for you at present," smiled his father. "Between the public, and the printer, and the book-binder the publisher is torn in many directions. And then there is the author, who, as I say, does not like his text tampered with.

Firms differ greatly about this. Some publishers feel perfectly justified in going ahead and remodeling a writer's work to suit themselves; others regard an author's manuscript as a sacred possession and never change so much as a punctuation mark on it without asking permission. They may suggest changes but they will not make them. It is a point of honor with them not to do so."

Mr. Cameron smoked reflectively.

"Authors, however," he went on, "are not as badly off as they were before they had the copyright. Their stories can no longer be stolen with impunity as in the past. They are better paid, too. Many an olden-time author received very scant remuneration for his labor; sometimes he received none at all. Many had to beg the patronage of the rich in order to get their works printed; contracts were unfair and publishers unprincipled. The unfortunate author was the prey of vultures who cheated him at every turn. Many died in extreme poverty, only to become famous when it was too late. In our day the law has revolutionized most of these injustices, and although there are still unprincipled publishers as there are always scamps in every calling, the best class houses deal honorably with their writers, transforming the relation between author and publisher into one of friendliness and confidence rather than one of animosity and distrust."

"I suppose it is policy for a publisher to be fair."

"It is more than policy; it is honesty," returned Mr. Cameron. "It does, however, pay, for without the writer the publisher could not exist, and no writer is going to put his work in the hands of a person he cannot trust. It is a short-sighted man who kills the goose that lays the golden egg!"

CHAPTER IX

PAUL EMBARKS ON ANOTHER VENTURE

"Do you know, Dad, the *March Hare* is rapidly turning into an elephant," announced Paul to his father one morning not long after the conversation of the previous chapter. "I am having more and more copy to prepare for Mr. Carter all the time, and am doing every bit of it by hand. It takes hours to get it ready. I'm beginning to think I ought to have a typewriter. How much does one cost? Have you any idea?"

"Typewriters come at all prices," his father answered. "What I should advise you to get would be one of the small, light-weight machines. They are far less expensive than the others and do excellent work."

"About how much would one cost?"

"Fifty or sixty dollars."

Paul gave a low whistle.

"That's all very well, sir," he laughed. "But where am I to get the fifty or sixty bones to pay for it?"

"I don't know, my boy. That's up to you. Doesn't your business manager provide you with a typewriter?"

"Not on your life!" replied Paul. "Much as ever I can wring enough money out of him to cover my incidental expenses. No, the paper isn't fitting up offices for its hard-working staff. If I get a typewriter it must be my own venture."

"You would always find such a machine useful," returned his father slowly. "It would not be money thrown away."

Paul glanced down thoughtfully.

"I've half a mind to save up and get one," he said suddenly. "I could put my war-saving stamps into it," he added.

"So you could."

"I have nearly twenty-five dollars' worth of them already."

"Oh, that's fine! I had no idea you had been so thrifty." Mr. Cameron looked pleased.

"We fellows have been racing each other up at school to see who could get his book filled first. I'm afraid it was not all thrift," Paul explained, meeting his father's eyes with honesty.

"The result, however, seems to be the same, whatever the motive," smiled the man. "Twenty-five dollars would be a splendid start toward a typewriter. You might possibly run across a second-hand machine that had not been much used and so get it for less than the regular price. I think, considering the cause is such a worthy one, I might donate ten dollars to it."

"Really! Oh, I say, Dad, that would be grand. I'll pick you right up on your offer."

"You may, son. I shan't pay over my ten dollars, though, until you have the rest of the money."

"That's all straight; only don't forget about it."

"You needn't worry. I don't expect you will give me the chance to forget even if I wanted to," replied his father teasingly.

"You bet I won't. I'm going right to work to get the rest of my cash as fast as I can," responded Paul. "And I'm going to look up machines, too."

"I can give you the names of one or two good makes," his father suggested.

"I wish you would, Dad. You think one of the small machines you spoke of would be good enough?"

"Certainly," assented Mr. Cameron. "Many persons who do a good deal of work use the little machines from preference. They take up less room and are lighter and more compact to carry about. In these days almost nobody is without a typewriter, especially persons who write to any considerable extent. Those who write for publication find a typewriter practically imperative. Editors will not fuss to decipher hand-penned copy. The time it takes and the strain on the eyes are too great. A professional writer must now turn in his manuscript neatly typed and in good form if he expects to have it meet with any attention. The old, blotted, finely written and much marked-up article is a thing of the past. Typewriters are so cheap in these days and so simply constructed that there is no excuse for people not owning and running them."

"I wonder who thought out the typewriter, Dad," mused Paul.

"That is a much mooted question, my boy," Mr. Cameron answered. "There is an old British record of a patent for some such device dated 1714, but the specifications regarding it are very vague and unsatisfactory; there also was an American patent taken out by William A. Burt as early as 1829. Fire, however, destroyed this paper and we have no positive data concerning it. Since then there have been over two thousand different patents on the typewriter registered at the Government Office at Washington,—so many of them that any person applying for a patent on a new variety must have a great deal of courage."

"I should say so!"

"Generally speaking, all typewriters resolve themselves into two styles of keyboard machine: in one the type bars strike the paper when the keys are depressed; in the other the type is arranged around a wheel which rotates in answer to the depressing of a keyboard letter, and prints the corresponding type which is thereby brought opposite the printing point. Either variety is good. It is a matter of preference. Possibly the type-bar kind is the more common. There is, too, a difference in the manner of inking the type. One machine inks the letters from an inked ribbon that is drawn along by the action of the machine between the type face and the paper; the type of the other machine is inked from an ink pad that strikes the type before it is brought in contact with the paper. Sometimes this ribbon or ink pad is black; sometimes blue, green, red, or purple. Sometimes, too, a ribbon is so constructed that it inks in two colors, which is frequently a convenience for business purposes. Text, for example, can be done in black and the numerals—prices perhaps—put in in red."

"I see. I should think that would be fine," said Paul. "Now tell me one other thing: are the letters arranged in the same order on all typewriters?"

"You mean the keyboards?"

"Yes, I guess that is what I mean," replied Paul.

"Keyboards sometimes differ in arrangement," Mr. Cameron explained. "Some keyboards have a key for each letter, and others one key for several characters. It is, however, desirable that machines should differ as little in arrangement as possible, as typists learn a universal method of letter-placing and are consequently annoyed to find the letters in an unfamiliar location on a new machine."

"I can see that would upset them dreadfully," answered Paul. "Of course they could not go so fast."

"Not only that, but they would make frequent mistakes," continued his father. "The most expert typists seldom look at the keys, you know. They memorize the position of the letters and then operate the machine by the touch system, or by feeling. You have often seen a person play the piano in the same fashion. It is a great advantage for a stenographer to be able to do this, for he can keep his eyes on his copy and not constantly change his eye-focus by glancing first at the manuscript and then at the machine. He can also give his entire attention to taking dictation if he so desires. The touch system is a great timesaver; it enables any one to make twice the speed."

"And the bell warns them that they are approaching the end of a line, even if they don't see that they are," Paul added.

"Precisely!"

"It is a great scheme, isn't it—a typewriter?" declared the boy. Mr. Cameron nodded.

"What wouldn't the old monks have given for one?" went on Paul mischievously. "Think of the years of work that would have saved them."

"Yes, that is true. But if we had no fine old illuminated manuscripts, we would have lost much that is beautiful and interesting. There is no question, though, that typewriters accord with our generation much more harmoniously than do painfully penned manuscripts. In our day the problem is to turn out the most work in the shortest time, and the typewriter certainly does that for us. It is a very ingenious device—a marvel until one sees a modern printing press; then the typewriter seems a child's toy, a very elementary thing indeed."

"I'd like to see a big press sometime," Paul observed. "I have been trying to get my nerve together to ask Mr. Carter for a permit to visit the *Echo* printing rooms."

"The *Echo*—humph!" laughed his father in derision. "Why, my boy, much as we esteem the *Echo* here in Burmingham, it is after all only a small local newspaper and very insignificant when compared with one of the big city dailies. You should visit the press rooms of a really large paper if you want to see something worth seeing. The *Boston Post*, for example, has the largest single printing press in the world. It was built in 1906 by the Hoe Company of New York and is guaranteed to print, count, fold, and stack into piles over 700,000 eight-page papers an hour."

"Great Scott, Dad!"

"It is tremendous, isn't it?"

"I'd like to see it."

"Sometime you shall. I think such a trip could be arranged," his father replied. "In the meantime I fancy you will have all you can do to earn the money for your typewriter, purchase it, and learn to manipulate it."

"I guess I shall; that's right," agreed Paul. "How am I going to get together the rest of that money! You haven't any suggestions, have you, sir?"

"Not unless you want to do Thompson's work while he takes his trip West. He is going out to Indiana to see his mother and will be away a month or so; in the meantime I have got to hire another man to do the chores about the place. The lawn must be cut; the leaves raked up; the driveway kept trim and in order; and the hedge clipped. If you want to take the job I will pay you for it."

"I'd have to do the work Saturdays, I suppose."

"That wouldn't hurt you, would it?"

Paul thought a moment.

"N—o."

"Undoubtedly it would interfere with your school games, the football and baseball," said his father. "Maybe a typewriter isn't worth that amount of sacrifice."

"Yes, it is."

"Think you want to make a try at Thompson's job?"

"Yes, sir."

"Then I won't hire in another man; only remember I shall expect you to stick to the bargain. I can't have you throwing up the place in a week or two."

"I shan't do that."

"And I can't have my work done haphazard, either," continued Mr. Cameron. "It must be done well and regularly."

"Yes, sir."

"You want me to give you a trial?"

"Yes, Dad."

"Do you want to do the whole job—the brasses indoors too?"

"Yes, I may as well take on the whole thing since I am out for money," laughed Paul.

"That's right. You have the proper spirit—the spirit that buys typewriters," answered his father. "I don't believe the exercise will hurt you, and at the end of it you will have something more to show than a dislocated shoulder, maybe, or a cracked cranium."

"Do you think I can earn what money I shall need to make up the rest of my fifty dollars?" inquired Paul anxiously. "Can I do it in a month?"

"A month of work will give you the rest of your fifty, son; have no fears. It will give you, too, all the work you will want for one while," answered Mr. Cameron. "Unless I am greatly mistaken, you will be quite ready to resign your post to Thompson when he comes back."

"Perhaps I shall," Paul replied, "but if you are repenting your bargain and are trying to scare me off, Dad, it is too late. You have hired me and I mean to stick it out."

"Go ahead, youngster, and good luck to you!" chuckled his father.

CHAPTER X

A DISASTER

It was after Paul had toiled early and late and put aside enough money for the new typewriter, and even a little more, that the first calamity befell the *March Hare.*

When the accounts were found to be short, it was unbelievable. Melville Carter, the business manager, who handled all the funds, was the soul of honesty as well as an excellent mathematician. His books were the pride of the editorial staff. Therefore when he was confronted with the hundred-dollar deficit, he could scarcely speak for amazement. There must be some mistake, he murmured over and over. He had kept the accounts very carefully, and not an expenditure had been made that had not been talked over first with the board and promptly recorded. There never had been a large surplus in the bank after the monthly bills were paid, but there was always a small margin for emergencies. The treasury had never before gone stone dry. But there it was! Not only was there no money in the bank, but the *March Hare* was about fifty dollars in the hole.

Paul and Melville went over and over the accounts, vainly searching for the error. But there was no error. The columns seemed to add up quite correctly. So, however, did the deposit slips from the bank. And the tragedy was that the two failed to agree. The bank had a hundred dollars less to the credit of the *March Hare* than the books said it should have.

In the meantime, at the bottom of Paul's pocket, lay a bill of fifty dollars for publishing expenses. What was to be done? The bill must be paid. It would never do to let the *March Hare* run behindhand. To begin to run into debt was an unsafe and demoralizing policy.

Paul's father had urged this advice upon him from the first. The *March Hare* must pay its bills as it went along; then its editors would know where they stood. And so each month the boys had plotted out their expenses and kept rigidly within the amount of cash they had in reserve. They had never failed once to have sufficient money to meet their bills. In fact, their parents had enthusiastically applauded their foresight and business ability.

And now, suddenly and unaccountably, here they were confronted by an empty treasury. What was to be done?

Of course the bill was not large. Fifty dollars was not a tremendous sum. But when you had not the fifty, and no way of getting it, the amount seemed enormous.

Then there was the balking enigma of it. How had it happened?

"If we only knew what we had done with that hundred, it would not be so bad," groaned Melville. "It makes me furious not to be able to solve the puzzle."

"Me, too!" Paul replied gravely.

And worse than all was the humiliation of finding they were not such clever business men as they had thought themselves to be. That was the crowning blow!

"A hundred dollars—think of it!" said Paul. "If it had been twenty-five! But a cool hundred, Mel!"

He broke off speechlessly.

"We can't be that amount short," protested Melville for the twentieth time. "We simply can't be. I have not paid one bill that the managing board has not first O.K.-ed. You know how carefully we have estimated our expenses each month. We have kept a nest-egg in the bank, too, all the time, in case we did get stuck. I can't understand it. We haven't branched out into any wild schemes. Of course, after the party we did make those presents to the school; but we looked over the ground and made sure that we could afford to do so."

"We certainly thought we could," returned Paul glumly. "Probably, though, we were too generous. Wouldn't people laugh if they knew the mess we are in now!"

"Well, they are not going to know it from me," growled Melville. "If I were to tell my father we were in debt he would say it was about what he expected. I wouldn't tell him for a farm down East. And how the freshmen would hoot!"

"I don't think my father would kid us," Paul said slowly, "but I know he would be awfully disappointed that we had made a business foozle."

"I, for one, say we don't tell anybody," Melville burst out. "I've some pride and I draw the line at having every Tom, Dick, and Harry shouting 'I told you so!' at me. What do you say, Paul, that we keep this thing to ourselves? If we have made a bull of it and got ourselves into a hole, let's get out of it somehow without the whole world knowing it."

"But how?"

"I don't know," Melville returned. "All I know is I'm not for telling anybody."

"But this bill, Melville? What is to become of that?"

"We must pay it."

"*We?*"

"You and I."

The room was very still; then Melville spoke again.

"Haven't you any ready money, Paul?"

"Y—e—s."

"Have you enough so that we could halve a hundred—pay the fifty-dollar deficit and put fifty dollars in the bank?"

"You mean you'd pay half of it if I would?"

"Yep."

"I—see."

"Could you manage it—fifty dollars?"

"Yes. Could you, Mel?"

"Well, I haven't the fifty; but I have a Liberty Bond that I could sell and get the money."

"That seems a shame," objected Paul.

"Oh, I don't care. I'm game. Anything rather than having the whole school twit me of messing the accounts."

"I don't care about being joshed, either," declared Paul. "Still—"

"Something's fussing you. What is it?"

"Well, you see, Mel, I've been doing extra work at home in order to earn enough money for a typewriter. I've just got it saved up. It'll have to go into this, now."

"Darned hard luck, old man! Don't do it if you don't want to. Maybe I can—"

"No, you can't! I wouldn't think of having you pay the whole hundred, even if you had the money right in your hand. This snarl is as much mine as yours. We probably haven't planned right. We've overlooked something and come out short."

"We might let the bill run until another month, I suppose," Melville presently suggested.

Paul started up.

"No. We mustn't do that on any account. We might be worse off another month. I say we clear the thing right up and start fair. If you will turn in your fifty, I will," declared he, with spirit.

"Bully for you! You sure are a sport, Kip."

"I don't see anything else to be done."

There was nothing else. Melville's "Baby Bond" was converted into cash; Paul's typewriter sacrificed; the fifty-dollar bill was paid; and the other fifty was put into the bank.

The boys kept their own council and if the *March Hare* sensed that its reputation had trembled on the brink of ruin it gave no sign. Gayly it went on its way.

People began to comment on the paper as being "snappy" and "up to date"; they called it "breezy" and "wholesome." Now and then an appreciative note from a distant graduate would make glad the editorial sanctum. Slowly, almost imperceptibly, the magazine became more and more the organ of speech for the community. Persons who had never ventured into print—who, perhaps, never would have ventured—summoned up courage to send to this more modest paper articles that were received with welcome. Being first efforts and words that their authors had long desired to speak they were stamped with a freshness and spontaneity that was delightful; if at times the form was faulty it was more than compensated for by the subject matter. Furthermore, many of the contributions were of excellent quality.

Then there gradually came a day when the timid *March Hare* had more desirable material than it had room to print. A part of this was political, for the school classes in current events had aroused in the students a keen interest in international affairs. As a consequence good political articles had been eagerly sought for. Other contributions were of scientific nature and appeared from time to time in the columns devoted to such matter. The great mass of material sent in, however, was unclassified and found its way into the department labeled: *Town Suggestions*; or into the pages known as: *Our Fathers and Mothers*. Neither of these departments had originally been featured in the *March Hare* plan; they came as a natural outgrowth of the paper. Parents had things which they wanted to say to one another or to their boys and girls. There was many a problem to be threshed out, threshed out more intimately than it could have been in a larger and more formal paper. The questions debated never failed to interest the elder part of Burmingham's population and frequently they appealed to the youngsters as well. In fact, it was not long before these departments were merged into a sort of forum where an earnest and vigorous interchange of opinions 'twixt young and old took place.

And all the while that the sprightly *March Hare* was thus leaping on to success, Mr. Arthur Presby Carter sat quietly in his office and watched the antics of this youthful upstart. He was surprised, very much surprised; indeed he had, perhaps, never been more surprised in all his life. He had long thought he knew a good deal about the make-up of a paper,—what would interest and what would not; in fact, he considered himself an expert in that sphere. He had put years of study into the matter. Even now he would not have been willing to confess that a seventeen-year-old boy had taught him anything. That would have been quite beneath his dignity. But privately he could not deny that this schoolboy adventurer had opened his eyes to a number of things he had never considered before.

The *Echo* was a conservative, old-fashioned paper that had followed tradition rather than the lead of an alert, progressive public. From a pinnacle of confident superiority it had spoken to the people, telling them what they should think, rather than giving ear to their groping and clamoring desire for a hearing. The *Echo* never discussed questions with its readers. Its editor had never deigned to do so, so why should his publication? To bicker, argue, and debate would have been entirely at odds with its standards. People did not need to state what opinions they held; they merely needed to be told what opinions they should hold. Thus thought Mr. Arthur Presby Carter, and thus had his policy been immortalized in his paper.

But now, to his amazement and chagrin, a publication had been born that was undermining his prestige and putting to naught his creeds and theories. This absurd *March Hare* was actually becoming the authorized mouthpiece of the town. It would have been blind not to recognize the fact. Fools had indeed rushed in where angels feared to tread, as Mr. Carter himself had jeeringly asserted they sometimes did, and as a result there had come into being this unique monthly whose subscription list was constantly swelling.

The publisher shrugged his shoulders. He was a shrewd business man. He had, he confessed to himself, been trapped into printing this amateur thing, and once trapped he had been game enough to live up to his contract; but he had always viewed the new magazine with a patronizing scorn. For a press of the *Echo's* reputation to be printing a silly High School publication had never ceased to be an absurdity in his eyes. He had regarded the first issues with derision. Then slowly his disdain had melted into astonishment, respect, admiration. There evidently was a spirit in Burmingham of which he had never suspected the existence,—an intelligence, an open-mindedness, a searching after truth. Hitherto the subscribers to any paper had been represented in his mind by a long list of names in purple ink, or else, by their money equivalent. Now, suddenly, these names became persons, voices, opinions. No one could take up the *March Hare* and not be conscious of a throbbing of hearts. It sounded through every page—that beating of hearts—fathers, mothers, girls, boys speaking with simple sincerity of the things they held dearest in their lives.

Why, it was a miracle, this living flesh and blood that glowed so warmly and sympathetically through the dead mediums of paper and ink!

How had the enchantment been wrought? the magnate asked himself. To be sure, he had never tried through the columns of the *Echo* to get into actual touch with those into whose homes his paper traveled. He had never cared who they were, what they thought, or how they lived. The problems puzzling their brains were nothing to him. But he now owned with characteristic honesty that had he cared to obtain from them this free expression of opinion and learn the reactions their minds were constantly reflecting, he would have been at a loss as to how to proceed.

Yet here, through the instrumentality of a mere boy, a boy the age of his own son, the elusive result had been accomplished!

Where lay the magic?

The *March Hare* was not a paper that could speak with authority on any subject, nor was it a magazine of distinct literary merit. On the contrary it naïvely confessed that it was young and did not know. It explained with frankness that it had not the wisdom to speak; that instead it merely echoed the thought of its readers.

It was this "echoing idea" that was new to Mr. Arthur Presby Carter. He had always spoken. To listen to the opinions of others he had considered tiresome. Very few persons had opinions that were worth listening to.

Nevertheless, after dissecting the reasons for the *March Hare's* popularity, and lopping off the minor elements of its uniqueness and wide appeal, the elder man faced the real psychological secret of the junior paper's success: it listened and did not talk; it was a dialogue instead of a monologue,—an exact reversal of his policy.

Moreover, this dialogue, contrary to his previous beliefs, presented amazingly interesting opinions. Here were the past and the present generation arguing on the policy of the new America,—what its government, its statesmanship, its ideals should be. The Past was rich in advice, experience; the Present in hope, faith, courage. Youth, the citizen of to-morrow, had a thousand theories for righting the nation's faults; and some of these theories were not wholly visionary.

Did his paper, Mr. Carter wondered, call out in the hearts and minds of those who read it a similar response of patriotism and high ideals? Did it reach the great human *best* that lies deep in every individual? Alas, he feared it did not. It was too autocratic. It aimed not to stimulate but to silence discussion and it probably did so, descending upon its audience with a confident finality that admitted of no argument.

The *March Hare*, on the other hand, was apologetically modest. Nobody quailed before it. Even the least of the intellectuals feared not to lift up his voice in its presence and demand a hearing.

Such a novel and rare product was worth perpetuating. From a money standpoint alone the paper might become in time a paying investment. It was, of course, a bit crude at present; but the kernel was there; so, too, was the long list of subscribers,—an asset to which he was not blind.

Suppose he was to buy out this schoolboy enterprise at the

end of the year and take it into his own hands? Might it not be nursed into a publication that would have a lasting place in the community and become a property of value?

He would improve it—that would go without saying—touch it up and polish it; doubtless he would think best to revise some of its departments; and—well, he would probably change its name and its cover design. He could not continue to perpetuate such an absurdity as that title. Perhaps he would christen it the *Burmingham Monthly*.

The notion of purchasing the amateur product appealed to his sense of humor. The more he thought of it, the stronger became his desire to own the paper. Strange he had never before considered publishing a monthly magazine. Yes, he would get out the few remaining issues of the *March Hare* under its present name and then he would buy out the whole thing for a small sum and take it over. The boys would undoubtedly be glad enough to sell it, flattered to have the chance, no doubt. A check that would provide the editorial staff with some hockey sticks or tennis shoes would without question satisfy them. What use would they have for a paper after they graduated?

Thus reasoned Mr. Arthur Presby Carter to himself in the solitude and silence of his editorial sanctum. And after he had disposed of the matter to his entire satisfaction, he took up a letter from his desk and decided with the same deliberation to purchase also certain oil properties in Pennsylvania. For Mr. Arthur Presby Carter was a man of broad financial interests and a large bank account. The Echo was only one of his many business enterprises, and buying *March Hares* or oil wells was all one to him, a means of adding more dollars to his accumulating hoard.

CHAPTER XI

TEMPTATION ASSAILS PAUL

While Mr. Carter sat in his editorial office and thus reflected on his many business ventures Paul Cameron was also sitting in his editorial domain thinking intently.

The hundred-dollar deficit in the school treasury bothered him more than he was willing to admit. It was, of course, quite possible for him to repair the error—for he was convinced an error in the *March Hare's* bookkeeping had caused the shortage. A bill of a hundred dollars must have been paid and not recorded. Melville Carter had never had actual experience in keeping accounts, therefore was it so surprising that he had inadvertently made a mistake? Perhaps he was not so capable of handling money and keeping it straight as the class had thought when they had elected him to his post of business manager. Paying bills and rigorously noting down every expenditure was no easy task. It was a thankless job, anyway—the least interesting of any of the positions on the paper, and one that entailed more work than most. To kick at Mel would be rank ingratitude. It was not likely he had made a mess of things wittingly. Therefore the only alternative, since neither Mel's pride nor his own would permit them to confess to the muddle, was to pay the outstanding bill and slip the rest of the cash as quietly as possible into the bank.

How strange it was that the sum lacking was just an even hundred dollars! Yet after all, was it so strange? It was so easy to make a mistake of one figure in adding and subtracting columns. There did not, it was true, seem to be any mistake on the books; but of course there was a mistake somewhere. It was not at all likely that the bank had made the error. Banks never made mistakes. Well, there was no use crying over spilled milk. The success of the *March Hare* had been so phenomenal hitherto that one must put up with a strata of ill luck.

He hated to give up buying his typewriter, after all the hard work he had done to earn it. He supposed he could sell his Liberty Bond as Melville was planning to do and use that money instead of the sum he had laid by. But he did not just know how to go to work to convert a Liberty Bond into cash. It was an easy enough matter to buy a bond; but where did you go to sell one? How many business questions there were that a boy of seventeen was unable to answer! If he were to ask his father how to sell the bond, it might arouse suspicion, to ask anybody else might do so too. People would wonder why he, Paul Cameron, was selling a Liberty Bond he had bought only a short time before. Burmingham was a gossipy little town. Its good news traveled fast but so also did its bad news. Any item of interest, no matter how small, was rapidly spread from one end of the village to the other. Therefore Paul could not risk even making inquiries, let alone selling his property to any one in the place.

Yet he could not but laugh at the irony of the signs that confronted him wherever he went: *Buy Bonds! Invest!* There were selling booths at the bank, the library, the town hall. At every street corner you came upon them. But none of these agencies were purchasing bonds themselves. Nowhere did it say: *Sell Bonds!* These patriots were not at their posts to add to their troubles—not they!

Once it occurred to Paul to ask the cashier at the bank what people did with Liberty Bonds which they wanted to dispose of; but on second thought he realized that Mr. Stacy was an intimate friend of his father's and might mention the incident. Therefore he at length dismissed the possibility of selling his bond and thereby meeting his share of the *March Hare* deficit.

No, he must use his typewriter money. There was no escape. He chanced to be at the *Echo* offices that day with copy for the next issue of his paper and was still rebelliously wavering over the loss of his typewriter when the door of Mr. Carter's private room opened and the great man himself appeared, ushering out a visitor. Glancing about on his return from the elevator his eye fell on Paul.

"Ah, Paul, good afternoon," he nodded. "Come into my office a moment. I want to speak to you."

Paul followed timidly. It was seldom that his business brought him into personal touch with Mr. Carter, toward whom he still maintained no small degree of awe; usually the affairs relative to the school paper were transacted either through the business manager of the *Echo* or with one of his assistants.

But to-day Mr. Carter was suddenly all amiability. He escorted Paul into his sanctum, and after closing the door, tipped back in the leather chair before his desk and in leisurely fashion drew out a cigar.

"How is your paper coming on, Paul?" he asked, as he blew a cloud of smoke into the room and surveyed the boy through its blueness.

"Very well, Mr. Carter."

"Austin, our manager, tells me your circulation is increasing."

"Yes, sir. It's gone up steadily from the first."

"Humph!" mused Mr. Carter. "Funny thing, isn't it? It was

quite a clever move of yours to set the parents to writing. Everybody likes to see himself in print; we're a vain lot of creatures. Of course, the minute you published their articles they bought them. Could not resist it!"

The lad laughed. Although he did not wholly agree with the editor it did not seem necessary to tell him so.

"I guess you've found your enterprise a good deal of work," went on Carter.

"Well, yes. It has taken more time than I expected," Paul admitted.

"You'll be glad to get rid of it when you graduate in June."

The man studied the boy furtively.

"Yes, I shall. It has been great fun; but it has been a good deal of care."

"You're going to Harvard, I hear."

"Yes, sir. Harvard was Dad's college, and it's going to be mine."

"I haven't much use for colleges," growled Mr. Carter. "They turn out nothing but a grist of extravagant snobs. I never went to college myself and I have contrived to pull along and make my pile, thanks to nobody. I've a big half mind to have Melville do the same. But his mother wants him to go, and I suppose I shall have to give in and let him. It will be interesting to see what he gets out of it."

Paul did not answer. He did not just know what reply to make.

"So you're set on college."

"Yes, sir, I am."

"What's your idea?"

"To know something."

The man's thin lips curled into a smile.

"And you expect to acquire that result at Harvard?"

"I hope so."

"Well, you may," remarked Mr. Carter, with a sceptical shrug of his shoulders, "but I doubt it. You will probably fritter away your time and your father's money in boat-racing, football, and fraternity dramatics; that is what it usually amounts to."

"It has got to amount to more than that with me," Paul declared soberly.

"Why?"

"Because Dad is not rich, and hasn't the money to throw away."

A silence fell upon the room.

"I should think that under those circumstances you would do much better to cut out a frilly education and go to work after you finish your high school course," observed the magnate deliberately. "Suppose I were to make you a good business offer? Suppose I were to take over that school paper of yours at the end of June—"

"What!"

"Wait a moment. Then suppose I took you in here at a good salary and let you keep on with this *March Hare* job? Not, of course, in precisely its present form but along the same general lines. We could make a paying proposition out of that paper, I am sure of it. It would need a good deal of improving," continued the great man in a pompous, patronizing tone, "but there is an idea there that could be developed into something worth while, unless I am very much mistaken."

"B—u—t—" stammered Paul and then stopped helplessly.

"The thing is not worth much as it now stands," went on Mr. Carter, puffing rings of smoke airily toward the ceiling, "but in time we could remodel it into a publication of real merit—make a winner of it."

Paul did not speak.

"How do you like newspaper work?" inquired Mr. Carter, shifting the subject adroitly.

"Very much—the little I've seen of it."

"If you were to come in here you might work up to a place on the *Echo*."

The boy started.

"You're a bright chap and I like you. I'd see you had a chance if you made good."

"You're very kind, sir, but—"

"Well, out with it! What's the matter?"

"It would knock my college career all—"

"Faugh! College career! Why, here is a career worth ten of it—the chance of a lifetime. I wouldn't offer it to every boy. In fact, I wouldn't offer it to any other boy I know of—not to my own son."

"It's very good of you, Mr. Carter."

"See here, youngster," said Mr. Carter, leaning toward Paul impressively, "when you are as old as I am you will learn that you've got to take opportunities when they come to you. The same one never comes twice. You don't want to turn down a thing of this sort until you've considered it from all sides. Think what it would mean to remodel that paper of yours with plenty of money behind you and put it on a footing with other professional magazines. That would be a feather in your cap! I could buy the *March Hare* in—"

"I'm not sure you could, Mr. Carter," replied Paul slowly. "The staff might not want to sell it."

"What!"

The tone was incredulous with surprise.

"I don't know that we fellows would feel that we had the

moral right to sell out," explained Paul quietly. "You see, although we have built up the paper it belongs to a certain extent to the school."

"Nonsense!" cut in Mr. Carter impatiently. "That's absurd! The publication was your idea, wasn't it?"

"Yes, at the beginning it was; but—"

"They wouldn't have had it but for you, would they?"

"I don't know; perhaps not," confessed the boy reluctantly.

"It was your project," insisted Carter.

"Yes."

"Then nobody has any right to claim it."

"Maybe not the right to really claim it. But all of us boys have slaved together to make it a success. It is as much their work as mine."

"What do they intend to do with it?"

"Pass it on to the school, I suppose. We haven't talked it over, though. We haven't got that far yet."

"Well, all I can say is that if you handed it over to the school free of charge you would be darn stupid. Why not make some money out of it? Offer to sell it to the school if you think you must; but don't give it away."

Paul shook his head dubiously.

"The school couldn't buy it. They've nothing to buy it with."

"Then you have a perfect right to sell it to somebody else," put in Mr. Carter quickly. "In the world of business, people cannot expect to get something for nothing. What you can't pay for you can't have. If the school has no money—" he broke off with a significant gesture. "Now if I offered you fellows a lump sum in June—a sum you could divide amongst you as you saw fit—wouldn't that be a perfectly fair and legitimate business deal?"

"I—I—" faltered Paul.

"Wouldn't it?" Mr. Carter persisted.

"I suppose so," murmured Paul unwillingly. "Only, you see, I still feel that the paper should go to the school. I think the other fellows would feel so too."

Nettled Mr. Carter rose and strode irritably across the room and back. Then he came to a standstill before Paul's chair and looked down with steely eyes into the lad's troubled face.

"But you admitted just now that you and the staff had made the paper what it is, didn't you?"

"Yes."

"Then it belongs to you, doesn't it?"

"In a certain sense; yes."

"Now see here, Paul," began Mr. Carter. "You are the editor-in-chief of that magazine, and the head of the bunch. What you say would go with them—or it ought to. You could make them think about what you pleased. Why don't you put it up to your staff to sell the paper to me and pocket the proceeds?"

"Because I don't think—"

"I guess you could manage to think as I wanted you to if it were worth your while, couldn't you?" smiled the great man insinuatingly.

"I don't quite—"

"Turn it over in your mind. It is a straight business proposition. You land your *March Hare* here in my office as my property at the end of June, and I will make it worth your while. Understand?" The great man eyed the lad keenly.

"Not fully, I'm afraid."

"But you would before I got through with you," chuckled Mr. Carter, rising.

Paul rose too. He was very glad to have the interview finished.

"We'll talk no more about this matter to-day," declared the editor lightly. "You think over carefully what I've said and come and see me again sometime."

"All right, sir."

Paul moved awkwardly toward the door. He wanted to add some word to conceal how worried, angry, and upset he really was, but he could think of nothing to say. It was ignominious to pass out of the room as if he were a whipped puppy. Men always terminated their business talks pleasantly, no matter how vexed they were with one another underneath.

He must show Mr. Carter that he also could close an interview in true man's fashion. His hand was on the knob of the door now; but he turned.

"Oh, by the way, Mr. Carter," he said with an off-hand air, "do you know where a person goes to sell a Liberty Bond?"

It was the only topic of conversation he could think of.

"Sell one?"

"Yes, sir." The boy blushed.

"In need of cash?"

"I—yes; I'm thinking of getting rid of a fifty-dollar bond I have."

"That's foolish. You'd much better keep it."

Paul shook his head with sudden resolve.

"I think if I can get rid of it without too much red tape, I'll let it go."

"Want the money badly, eh?"

"Y—e—s."

"Your father know you are selling out?"

"No, sir."

The boy began to regret that he had spoken.

"Oh—ho! So you're in a scrape, eh?"

"BUT I CAN'T TAKE YOUR MONEY, MR. CARTER," GASPED PAUL.

"No, it's not a scrape," protested Paul. "At least, not what you'd commonly call a scrape. It is just that—"

"That you do not want to tell your father."

"Not now."

Mr. Carter winked.

"I see," he said.

He went to a drawer in his desk and innocently Paul watched his movements, wondering what he was going to do. Give him an address where he could sell his bond, no doubt.

Instead Mr. Carter slipped a crisp bill from a roll in the drawer and held it toward him.

"I'll advance you fifty dollars on your bond," he said, "and no questions asked. I was a boy once myself."

"But I can't take your money, Mr. Carter," gasped Paul, trying to hand the crackling bit of paper back again.

"Pooh, pooh! Nonsense!" the man ejaculated, waving him off. "Call it a loan if you prefer. A loan with a bond for security is quite an ordinary business matter. It is only a trifle, anyway."

"But—"

"Run along! I have no more time to give to you. I have a directors' meeting at four. Ah, here's Mr. Dalton now. How are you, Dalton. Run along, youngster. Take the cash with you and welcome." Then he added in an undertone: "Just use your influence with your chums up at school, and we will say no more about this little loan. If you land the *March Hare* in my hands the deal will be worth the fifty to me. Good night."

CHAPTER XII

TEMPORIZING

It was not until Paul was on his way home that the full significance of Mr. Carter's action dawned upon him. He, Paul Cameron, had been bribed! He had taken from the magnate of Burmingham a sum of money in return for which he had tacitly pledged himself to use his influence to carry through a business deal which he held to be wrong, and with which he had no sympathy. To be sure, he had not done this monstrous deed voluntarily. Mr. Carter had thrust it upon him. He had been put in a difficult position and had failed to act. It was his passivity for which he now blamed himself. He should have repudiated the whole thing, hurled the odious money upon Carter's desk—since the man refused to take it back—and fled from the place. The fact that Mr. Carter had given him no opportunity to discuss the matter or refuse his offer was no excuse. He should have made the opportunity himself.

The only apology he could offer for his conduct was that he was completely stunned by the happenings of the afternoon. The drama had moved too swiftly for him. Until it was over, he had not sensed its trend. Was he really so much to blame?

Nevertheless, twist and excuse the fact as he would, the truth remained that there he was with the hateful fifty-dollar bill in his possession.

It was appalling, terrible! He, who had always prided himself on his honesty! He had not had the least notion of precipitating such a crisis when he had inquired about selling his Liberty Bond. The query had been a purely innocent one. He had to say something, and the chance of getting information from Mr. Carter had seemed too opportune to let slip. But as he reviewed the episode of the past half hour, he saw that Mr. Carter was perfectly justified in misunderstanding him and thinking that he laid himself open to the very situation that had come about.

Paul fingered the bill nervously. Fifty dollars! If he chose to use it to meet the deficit on the school paper he could now take his own savings for the new typewriter he wanted so much. Who would be the wiser? Had not Mr. Carter given him the money? It was his, his own property.

To forfeit that typewriter had been a wrench. He had not dared to admit to himself how bitter had been his disappointment at giving it up. It would be a long time before he could ever again earn enough money to buy a machine. And he needed it so much—needed it right away. Suppose he did buy a typewriter next year? A dozen typewriters would never mean to him what one would mean just now. Until he had made up his mind to do without it, it had seemed an indispensable possession, and now the necessity of having it came back again with redoubled force. He reflected on the machine's myriad advantages. Wasn't it almost imperative that he buy one? Wasn't such a thing for the welfare of the school? Surely it would not be a selfish action if he expended his money for the good of others.

Suppose he were to urge the fellows to sell out the *March Hare* to Carter? After all, they were their own masters. They need not do so unless they chose. He had no authority over them. To advise was a very different thing from commanding.

No matter what measure he advocated, his opinion was neither final nor mandatory. He was no autocrat or imperator before whose decree his subjects trembled. It would be absurd to credit himself with such power.

And, anyway, the editorial board had never promised to bequeath the *March Hare* to the school. If parents, teachers, pupils, the general public had assumed this, they had had no right to do so. The paper, as Mr. Carter had said, was the property of those who had created it. Were they not free to dispose of it as they chose?

Yet all the while he argued thus, Paul knew, deep down in his soul, that although there had been no written or verbal agreement, the community considered the publication a permanent school property.

Should it be sold to Mr. Carter and continue to be published, what chances for success would another such paper have? It would be useless for 1921 to attempt to duplicate the *March Hare*. People were familiar with it; they knew and liked it. In all probability a great portion of its regular subscribers would continue to take the magazine, regardless of who published it. That it had ceased to be a school enterprise would not influence them. They liked it for what it was, not as a philanthropy. Probably, too, with Mr. Carter behind it, the *March Hare* would branch out and be made much more attractive. If the *Echo* press took up the publication of such a monthly, it would, of course, be with the intention of sweeping all other competitors out of the field. It *would* sweep them out, too. Mr. Carter would see to that. By fair means or foul he had always accomplished that which he willed to do.

Another school paper running in opposition to such a power? Why, it would not have the ghost of a chance to live! Besides, who would print it? No, if Mr. Carter took over the *March Hare,* the school must say good-by to further literary attempts.

But after all, was that his lookout? What concern of his would it be what became of Burmingham and 1921. They could struggle on as best they might. That was what his class had had to do.

Paul walked home very slowly, turning Mr. Carter's bill in his hand as he went. How delicate its workmanship! How wonderful its dainty tracery! He had never before noticed the accuracy with which a bill was fashioned.

"Who prints United States money, Dad?" he asked quite irrelevantly of his father, when next he saw him.

"Our United States greenbacks? Those are engraved and printed, my son, at the United States Bureau of Engraving and Printing at Washington. They are made from very fine and exquisitely prepared plates and printed on a special sort of paper. This paper has numberless little silk threads running through it which not only toughen it and prevent it from tearing but also make it almost impossible to duplicate. A counterfeiter would have to go to a deal of trouble to imitate such material."

Paul nodded. He had noticed the blue threads in his fifty-dollar bill. In fact, there was not much about it that he had not noticed while twisting and turning it in his fingers.

"Yes," continued his father, "our paper money and government notes are fine examples of accurate and perfect workmanship. I suppose, as they pass through our hands, we seldom consider the labor that goes into making them. From the time the designer begins his work to the moment the plates are made, tried out, and accepted, many, many hours of toil are consumed. You know, of course, that our government runs a very extensive printing plant where it uses tons of paper every year. There is no end to the government printing. The Congressional Records must be printed and filed, as must also thousands of reports from various boards and committees. Then there is stationery for official use; official documents of all sorts; catalogues; cards for government business."

"I never thought of that."

"Yes, indeed. Uncle Sam runs quite a jobbing office, all the details of which must be carefully systematized, too. Great care is taken that the spelling abbreviations and such details shall be uniform on all government documents. You can readily see how necessary it is that they should be. Therefore the government issues a manual for the use of its employees, a list of punctuation and capitalization marks and rules, as well as printers' marks which shall serve as a standard and must be conformed to for all government purposes."

"That is interesting, isn't it?" murmured Paul.

"You can readily understand that in preparing government reports and such things for the press a uniform abbreviation for the States, for example, must be used. It would be out of the question to have one person abbreviating Alabama one way and another person another. It would not only result in a slipshod lot of documents but the variation might mislead those who read it. In all such documents every detail must be the same. Moreover, often employees are far from being expert in such matters and a book to which they can refer is a great help to them. In addition, it settles all disputes arising between the clerks who make up the reports and the printers who print them; and it saves the time and labor of correcting errors."

"I see."

"Not only does the government printing office do a vast amount of printing for the use of the Washington authorities but it does a great deal of work for the country at large. Think, for instance, of the care and accuracy that goes into making out the United States census."

"Not only care but paper and ink," laughed Paul.

"All such tabulated documents consume quantities of paper," answered his father. "Directories, telephone books, circulars, and advertising matter in general demand tons and tons of paper every year, and the printing of them provides employment for hundreds of printers. As time goes on, more and more business is annually transacted by mail. The country is so tremendous and the expense of sending out salesmen to cover it so great that merchants now do much of their selling from mail-order catalogues. Many of these books are very attractive, too. A careful reproduction of the object for sale is made and the photograph sent broadcast to speak for itself. Jewelry firms issue tempting lists of their wares; china and glass dealers try to secure buyers by offering alluring pages of pictures, many of them in color; dry goods houses send out photographs of suits, hats, and clothing of all sorts. You have seen scores of such books and know how they are indexed and priced. In fact, there are commercial firms whose mail-order department is a business in itself, catalogues entirely supplanting salesmen. It is a much cheaper, wider-reaching means of selling, and often the results are quite as good as are the more old-fashioned methods. Now that artistic cuts can be reproduced with comparatively little expense this means of advertising is becoming more and more popular. Many charities annually make their appeal for funds by leaflet or card; stocks are offered to customers; your patronage to theaters, entertainments, and hotels is thus solicited. The combination of low postage rates and wide mail distribution is accountable for an almost overwhelming amount of printed business being transacted. Then, too, the mail is a great timesaver, or should be, an advantage to be considered in our busy, work-a-day world."

"But people don't read half the stuff they get through the mails," said Paul.

"No, of course not. If they did, they would do little else," smiled his father. "Nevertheless, they glance at it and now and then, as their eye travels over it, an item on the page catches their fancy. Any artistic advertisement will usually command attention; so will the receipt of some trifling article that is pretty or novel. Besides, it is chiefly the rushed city person who tosses the advertisement away unread. Those with more leisure, country people, perhaps, who receive little mail, usually read every word of the printed matter that reaches them. They do not have so many diversions as we do, and this printed stuff entertains them and keeps them in touch with the cities. Therefore they generally go over what is sent them quite carefully. Frequently they are miles from large shops and are forced to do much of their purchasing by mail, so such catalogues are a great convenience to them."

"I can see that," Paul admitted.

"Yes, indeed. Catalogues to those living in sparsely settled districts are a profound blessing. I should not be surprised to see the paper, ink, and printing business one of our largest industries. We cannot do without any of these commodities. Have you thought, for example, of the amount of material and labor that goes into producing the millions of thick telephone directories annually circulated among the subscribers? All these have to be printed somewhere."

"It must be an awful piece of work to get them out, Dad."

"It is. They must be printed absolutely correctly too, for an error will cause both the exchange and the subscriber no end of trouble. So it is with residence directories and many similar lists. If you consider, you can readily see that as a nation we consume an unbelievable amount of paper and ink in a year. That is why the shortage of these materials during the war caused such universal inconvenience. And not only do we demand a great deal of paper, and ink, and printer's skill in every department of our business, but being a country alert for education, we annually use a tremendous number of schoolbooks. Hundreds, thousands, millions of schoolbooks are printed each year for the purpose of educating and democratizing our growing citizens."

Paul stirred in his chair uneasily. The talk had drifted back into the familiar channels of the present. Again the school, Mr. Carter, the fifty-dollar bill, and the thoughts that for the instant had taken flight now returned to his mind, bringing a cloud to his face.

His father, noticing the shadow, looked kindly into the boy's eyes.

"You are tired to-night, son," he said.

"A little."

"Not working too hard?"

"No, sir. I don't think so."

"Everything going all right at school?"

"Yes."

"Paper still booming?"

"Yes, Dad. Going finely."

"I am glad to hear that."

Mr. Cameron waited a second. A wild impulse to take his father into his confidence seized Paul. He hesitated. Then it was too late. His father rose and with a friendly touch on his shoulder strode across the hall and into his den.

"You must not overwork at your editorial desk, my boy," he called jocosely from the distant threshold. "It doesn't pay."

Paul heard the door slam. The moment for confession had passed. His father had gone and he was alone with his conscience and Mr. Carter's fifty-dollar bill.

CHAPTER XIII

THE CAMERONS HAVE A VISITOR

During the next week Paul was obliged to go several times to the *Echo* offices and each time he went with the secret hope that he would see Mr. Carter and have the opportunity to hand back to him the hateful money that burned in his breast pocket. The chance, however, never came. The door of the great man's private room was continually closed and when the boy suggested to the clerk that he wait and talk with the publisher, he was told that Mr. Carter was engaged and could see no one that day. The thought of mailing the money occurred to Paul, but as this method of returning it seemed precarious and uncertain, he promptly abandoned the idea. For the same reason he was unwilling to leave the bill in a sealed envelope to be delivered to the editor-in-chief by one of the employees. Should a sum so immense, at least so immense in the lad's estimation, be lost, he never could replace it. Certainly he was in trouble enough already without chancing another dilemma.

In the meantime he carried the bill around with him, trying in the interval to decide what to do with it. Gradually he became accustomed to having the money in his possession. It did not seem so strange a thing now as it had in the beginning. After all, fifty dollars was not such a vast sum. To a person of

Mr. Carter's wealth it probably was nothing at all, an amount too trifling to cause a second thought. Besides, he had not really bound himself to Mr. Carter. He had not actually guaranteed to do anything. It was Mr. Carter who had insisted that he take the money.

Unquestionably in exchange for it Paul was expected to use his influence to persuade the boys of 1920 to sell their paper; still, using one's influence did not necessarily mean that one must succeed. If he suggested the deal and it failed to go through, would he not have done all that was required of him? Mr. Carter had stipulated nothing more than that he use his influence. If the *Echo* owner had over-estimated the power of that influence, was not that his lookout? No doubt such an understanding was quite customary in business circles and was not so important a matter as he took it to be.

The more the lad thought the matter over the more plausible the retention of the money seemed. To use one's influence was surely a legitimate arrangement. It was done in politics every day of the week. Weren't individuals in high positions constantly accepting tips to put through business measures of one sort or another, regardless of whether they personally approved of them or not? To be sure, he had heard his father call such money *bribe money, dirty money,* and refer to the men who took it as being *bought up.*

Paul knew his father scorned such proceedings. That was the reason he had lost the campaign when running for mayor against Mr. Carter in 1915. It had been an underhanded fight and almost everyone in Burmingham, regardless of party, had thought so. Mr. Carter had won the election, it is true, but it had been at the expense of the respect of the entire community.

And now he, Paul Cameron, was deserting the principles for

which his father stood and was accepting those of his opponent. Plainly speaking, that was what the thing amounted to. He was taking money for something he disapproved of doing; he was being a traitor to his class, to his friends, to the school. The boys on the staff of the paper respected and trusted him. They would never suspect him of treachery. Should he stand up and advocate the sale of the *March Hare* he knew his word would have weight. If, on the other hand, he manfully presented Mr. Carter's offer as it honestly should be presented, he was practically sure that the measure would be voted down.

Yet if he returned the money to Mr. Carter and refused to have anything further to do with the affair, he must forfeit his typewriter, the thing on which he had set his heart.

What an unlucky snarl it was! How unfortunate that the *March Hare's* bank account should have been muddled and its editor driven to repair an error that was not his! Had not this occurred, all would have gone smoothly and he could have thrust the odious money back in Mr. Carter's face and left his office a free man. He hated Mr. Carter, the *March Hare,* the school, and all the web of circumstances in which he was entangled! He wanted that typewriter. It seemed as if he must have it. In the meantime, the May issue of the school paper came out and preparations for the June number, the last that 1920 would publish, began. The swift passing of the days forced Paul's hand. Whichever way he was to act he must act soon now, and he found himself no nearer a decision than he had been two weeks ago. He still had Mr. Carter's money in his pocket, and he was still eyeing the Corona he longed for and which he could neither bring himself to purchase nor give up; he was, too, quite as unreconciled to doing his Alma Mater an injury as he had been before. Round and round in a circle he went, the same old arguments bringing him to the same old conclusions. There seemed to be no way out.

While he was still pondering what he would do, an interesting visitor arrived at the Cameron home. This was Mr. Percy Wright, a college classmate of Paul's father and the owner of one of the largest paper mills in the State. He was a man of magnetic personality and wide business experience and Paul instantly conceived that warm admiration for him which a younger boy will often feel for an older man.

A fund of amusing anecdotes rippled from Mr. Wright's tongue. It seemed as if there was no subject on which he could not converse. He had an entertaining story about almost every topic suggested and kept the entire Cameron family laughing heartily through each meal. Paul watched the stranger with fascinated eyes. How charming he was, how witty, how clever! And yet Mr. Wright was not always jesting. On the contrary, he could be very serious when his hobby of paper-making, with its many interdependent industries, was mentioned.

He was, for example, in close touch with the publication of periodicals, newspapers, and books, and he immediately hailed Paul as a colleague.

"So you are the editor-in-chief of a widely circulated monthly magazine, are you, my boy?" he remarked. "Well, you certainly have an enviable job. It is a pity you are not going to keep on with the work. Your father tells me he thinks you have made a great success of it."

Paul colored uncomfortably.

"Not that I would have you throw over your college career," added Mr. Wright quickly. "Not for a moment! But publishing work is so alluring! I have always wanted to own a newspaper and I have not yet given up hope of doing so before I die."

"My paper isn't anything wonderful," said Paul modestly.

"But it is a clean, good magazine of its sort. I have been looking over several copies of it since I have been here. You have nothing to be ashamed of. I call the *March Hare* a mighty fine little publication. It's a splendid starter and I'll be bound has given you some excellent experience. Every paper has to have a beginning. All our big newspapers began on a small scale. There is some difference between one of our modern Sunday issues and the *Boston News-Letter* of long ago."

"I don't think I know what the *Boston News-Letter* was," Paul said.

"You've never seen a copy of this early Massachusetts newspaper?"

"No, sir."

"Well, it was a small, four-page sheet, printed in old type, and filled to a great extent with announcements of merchandise that had been shipped from England to the colonies for sale: pipes of wine, bolts of homespun, pieces of silk, consignments of china. Such things came from overseas in those days, and the arrival of the vessels that brought them was eagerly awaited by prospective purchasers, for there were few luxuries in the New World. Along with these advertisements was printed the news of the day; and that all this matter could be contained in four small pages proves how uneventful was early Massachusetts history. Now and then some great event would command more space. I recall seeing one copy of the paper with a picture of the first steam locomotive—a crude, amusing picture it was, too. Later the *Massachusetts Gazette* appeared, and soon afterward there were other papers and other printers scattered throughout the respective States. Benjamin Franklin was in Boston, you remember, from 1723 until 1726, when he went to Philadelphia and did publishing work until 1756. A hand press identical in principle with the one he used is still preferred to this day in the large newspaper press rooms for striking off proof when the amount of it is too small to be put through a power press. The hand press is a simple and quick agent for getting a result. The ink roller is run over the type and hand pressure is applied. One could not of course print a large newspaper on such a limited scale; but for jobbing work Franklin's variety of press is still acceptable and unrivaled."

"It seems funny to think of a Boston paper ever being so small," mused the boy.

Mr. Wright smiled.

"And not only small but of infrequent issue," said the paper manufacturer. "In 1709 there was only one daily paper published in London; twelve appeared three times a week; and three twice a week."

"Great Scott!"

"Yes, it is amazing, isn't it? *The Tatler* began in 1709 and *The Spectator* not long afterward. You must recall that the entire newspaper industry as we know it has been developed within comparatively recent years. The great daily, with its Sunday edition of pictures, colored sheets, news of classified varieties, and advertising and sporting sections, is only possible by means of the modern press which has the capacity for turning out in a short time such an immense number of papers."

Paul listened, fascinated by the subject.

"Gradually," went on Mr. Wright, "new brains attacked the problems of the small press, improving and enlarging it until little by little a press was built up which is so intricate and so wonderful that it almost ceases to be a machine and becomes nearly human. Boston, you know, harbors the largest printing press in the world. It is made up of 383,000 parts; it carries eight huge rolls of paper weighing from thirteen hundred to fifteen hundred pounds, four of them at each end; and in addition it has two color presses attached on which the colored supplement is printed."

"How do they ever lift such heavy rolls of paper into place?" inquired Paul.

"A chain is put around them and they are hoisted up by machinery," answered Mr. Wright. "The employees are warned to stand from under, too, when they are lifted, for should one of those mighty rolls fall, the person beneath might be seriously injured or perhaps killed."

"How many papers can they turn out on a press of that size?" was Paul's next question.

"It is possible to turn out 726,000 eight-page papers an hour or the equivalent of that quantity; the number of papers depends on the size of them, you see."

"What do you suppose good Benjamin Franklin would say to that?" laughed Paul.

"I fancy he would remark a number of things," Mr. Wright returned. "In fact, a modern newspaper plant, with its myriad devices for meeting the business conditions of our time, would be quite an education to Franklin, as it is to the rest of us. Did you ever see a big newspaper printed from start to finish, Paul?"

"No, sir."

"Ah, that's a pity. As a publisher you should be better informed on your subject," observed the elder man half teasingly. "I am going to Boston on Saturday. If your father is willing would you like to go along with me and spend the week-end in town?"

The lad's eyes shone.

"Would I like it!" he managed to stammer.

"I've got to see some of the business houses we supply with paper," continued Mr. Wright, "and incidentally I am sure I could arrange a visit to a big newspaper office Saturday evening when they are getting out the Sunday papers and have all their presses in operation."

"That would be great!"

"I think you would enjoy the trip," asserted Mr. Wright. "The printing of a paper is a wonderful process to see. I have a great admiration and respect for a fine newspaper, anyway. When one considers how widely it is read and the influence it possesses for good or evil, one cannot but take off his hat to it. No agency in the community can more quickly stir up or allay strife. Public opinion to no small extent takes its cue from the papers. They are great educators, great molders of the minds of the rank and file. Let the papers whisper war or national calamity and the stock markets all over the world are affected. And that is but one of the vital influences the paper wields. The temper of the whole people is colored by what they read. Whenever the editorials of reputable papers work toward a specific goal, they usually achieve it. Have we not had a striking example of that during the present war? The insidious power of propaganda is incalculable. Fortunately our national papers are high-minded and patriotic and have directed their influence on the side of the good, quieting fear, promoting loyalty, encouraging honesty, and strengthening the nobler impulses that govern the popular mind. For people are to an extent like a flock of sheep; they give way to panic very quickly. What one thinks the next one is liable to believe. Much of this opinion is in the hands of the newspapers. At the same time, the minds of the greater thinkers of the country are often clarified by reading the opinions mirrored by the press. One cannot praise too highly the wisdom and discretion of our newspapers during the perilous days of war when a word from them might have been as a match to tinder, and when they held many important secrets in their keeping. The great dailies were loyal to the last degree and the confidence that was placed in them was never betrayed. It was unavoidable that they should possess knowledge that the rest of us did not; but they never divulged it when cautioned that to do so would be against the national welfare. The sailings of ships, the departure of troops, the names of the ports from which vessels left, the shipment of food and supplies—all tidings such as these the press withheld."

"It was bully of them!" Paul exclaimed with enthusiasm.

"Yes, they rendered a great service. And you must remember that it was especially difficult since there is always a keen rivalry between papers and a tremendous eagerness to be the first one with the news. Whenever a paper gets inside information of an interesting nature there is a great temptation to publish it. There have been few such offenses, however, during the present war, be it said to the newspaper men's credit. Hence it became possible for the President to grant regular interviews to the leading reporters of the country and speak to them with comparative frankness with regard to national policies without fear that what he said would be garbled and turned to mischievous ends."

"I don't believe I ever thought before of the responsibility the papers had," remarked Paul soberly.

"Their responsibility is immeasurable," replied Mr. Wright. "The opportunity a paper has for checking rash judgment and arousing the best that is in humanity is endless. That is why I should like to control a newspaper, that I might make it the mouthpiece of all that is highest and noblest. To my mind only persons of splendid ideals should be entrusted with the publishing of papers. If the editor is to form the opinion of the masses, he should be a man worthy of his mission."

Paul toyed with his cuff-link.

"So, son," concluded Mr. Wright, "you've got to be a very good person if you aim to be a newspaper man—at least, that's what I think. Any printed word is like seed; it is liable to take root you know not where. A paper voices the thought of those who produce it. Therefore it behooves its makers to consider well their thoughts."

The boy winced and a flush surged to his forehead. Certainly Mr. Wright would not approve of the fifty-dollar bill which at that instant lay concealed in his pocket. As he turned to leave the room, he was very conscious of the leather pocketbook that pressed against his heart. He wished he was clear of that money. But he had already kept it more than two weeks and it was of course too late to return it now.

CHAPTER XIV

PAUL MAKES A PILGRIMAGE TO THE CITY

The trip to Boston which Mr. Wright suggested materialized into quite as delightful an excursion as Paul had anticipated. In fact, it was an eventful journey, filled with every variety of wonderful experience.

The elder man and his young guest arrived in the city Friday night in plenty of time to enjoy what Paul called *a great feed* and afterward go to a moving-picture show. It was odd to the suburban boy to awake Saturday morning amid the rumble and roar from pavements and crowded streets. But there was no leisure to gaze from the window down upon the hurrying throng beneath, for Mr. Wright was off early to keep a business engagement and during his absence Paul was to go to the circus. Accordingly the lad hurried his dressing and was ready to join his host for breakfast promptly at eight.

A league baseball game followed after lunch and with a morning and an afternoon so crammed with pleasure Paul would have felt amply repaid for the trip had no evening's entertainment followed. The evening, however, turned out to be the best part of the day; at least, when Paul tumbled into bed that night, wearied out by his many good times, he asserted that the crowning event of his holiday had given him more interesting things to think about.

It was not until nine o'clock Saturday evening that they could go to the newspaper office.

"Before that hour," explained Mr. Wright, "there will be very little for us to see. The compositors, of course, will previously have been busy setting type; but you can get an idea how that is done in a very short time. What I want you to see are the giant presses when they are running to their full capacity. To get out the Sunday edition of the paper the entire plant is in operation."

Therefore the two travelers loitered long at dinner and at nine o'clock presented themselves at the magic spot where they were to meet one of Mr. Wright's friends who was to show them through the various departments of the press plant.

When they reached this Eldorado, however, Paul was disappointed.

The manager's office seemed very quiet. A dim light burned and a few men moved in and out of the adjacent rooms. Now and then a telephone jangled, or a reporter, perched on the arm of a chair or on the corner of a desk, took out a yellow sheet of paper and ran his eye over its contents. But there was none of the bustle and rush that the lad had pictured. But before Paul had had time to become really downhearted, the door of an inner office opened and a man came forward to meet them.

"Ah, Wright, I'm glad to see you!" he called, extending his hand.

"I'm glad to see you too, Hawley. I expect we're making you a deal of trouble and that you wish us at the bottom of the Dead Sea."

"Not a bit of it!"

"That's mighty nice of you," laughed Mr. Wright. "I give you my word, I appreciate it. This is my young friend Paul Cameron, the editor-in-chief of the Burmingham *March Hare*."

If Mr. Hawley were ignorant of the *March Hare's* existence or speculated at all as to what that unique publication might be, he at least gave no sign; instead he took Paul's hand, remarking gravely:

"I am glad to know you, Cameron," upon the receipt of which courtesy Cameron rose fully two inches in his boots and declared with equal fervor:

"I am glad to meet you too, Mr. Hawley."

To have seen them one would have thought they had been boon companions at press club dinners or associates in newspaper work all their days. "I'm going to take you upstairs first," Mr. Hawley said briskly. "We may as well begin at the beginning and show you how type is set. I don't know whether you have ever seen any type-making and typesetting machines or not."

"I haven't seen anything," Paul confessed frankly.

The newspaper man looked both amused and pleased.

"I'm rather glad of that," he remarked, "for it is much more interesting to explain a process to a person to whom it is entirely new. Formerly the method of setting type for the press was a tedious undertaking and one very hard on the eyes; but now this work is all done, or is largely done, by linotype machines that place in correct order the desired letters, grouping them into words and carefully spacing and punctuating them. The linotype operator has before him a keyboard and as he presses the keys in succession, the letter or character necessary drops into its proper place in the line that is being made up. These letters are then cast as they stand in a solid, one-line piece. With the lines thus made up, the compositors are relieved of a great proportion of their labor. Later I will show you how this is done.

"In the composing room there is also the monotype, another ingenious invention, which produces single letters and prepares them for casting. With two such machines you might suppose that the compositor would have little to do. Nevertheless, in spite of each of these labor-saving devices, there are always odd jobs to be done that cannot be performed by either of these agencies; there are short articles, the making up and designing of pages, advertisements, and a score of things outside the scope of either linotype or monotype."

Paul listened attentively.

"After the words have been formed and the lines cast by the linotype, the separate lines are arranged by the compositors inside a frame the exact size of the page of the paper to be printed. This frame or form as we call it, is divided into columns and after all the lines of type, the cuts, and advertisements to be used are arranged inside it, so that there is no waste space, a cast is made of the entire form and its contents. This cast is then fitted upon the rollers of the press, inked, and successive impressions made from it. This, in simple language, is what we are going to see and constitutes the printing of a paper."

Paul nodded.

"Of course," continued Mr. Hawley, "we shall see much more than that. We shall, for example, see how cuts and advertisements are made; photographs copied and the plates prepared for transfer to the paper; color sheets in process of making; in fact, all the varied departments of staff work. But what I have told you are the underlying principles of the project. I want you to understand them at the outset so that you will not become confused."

"I think I have it pretty straight," smiled Paul.

"Very well, then; we'll get to work."

"Not that I thoroughly understand how all this is done," added the boy quickly. "But I have the main idea and when I see the thing in operation I shall comprehend it more clearly, I am sure. You see, I don't really know much of anything about printing a paper. All I am actually sure of is that often the making up of a page is a big puzzle. I've had enough experience to find that out."

"That is sometimes a puzzle for us, too," smiled Mr. Hawley. "Fitting stuff into the available space is not always easy. Usually, however, we know just how many words can be allowed a given article and can make up our forms by estimating the mathematical measurement such copy will require. When the type is set in the forms, so accurately cut are the edges, and so closely do the lines fit together, the whole thing can be picked up and held upside down and not a piece of its mosaic fall out. That is no small stunt to accomplish. It means that every edge and corner of the metal type is absolutely true and exact. If it were not, the form would not lock up, or fit together. The letters, too, are all on the same level and the lines parallel. Geometrically, it is a perfect surface."

"Some picture puzzle!" Mr. Wright observed merrily.

"One better than a jigsaw puzzle," said Mr. Hawley. "Our pieces are smaller."

The three visitors stepped from the elevator and paused at the door of a crowded room, where many men were at work.

"These are the composing rooms," explained Mr. Hawley. "Here the copy sent us by reporters and editors is set up for the press. Along the walls you will see tiers of drawers in which type of various kinds and sizes is kept. The style or design of letter is called the 'face', and there are a great many sorts of faces, as you will notice by the labels on the drawers. There is Cheltenham, Ionic, Gothic—a multitude of others. There are, in addition, almost as many sizes of letters as there are faces, the letters running from large to a very small, or agate size which is used for footnotes."

He opened a drawer and Paul glanced inside it.

"But the letters do not seem to be arranged with any system at all," exclaimed the boy in surprise. "I don't see how the men can ever find what they want. I should think—"

He broke off, embarrassed.

"You should think what?" asked Mr. Hawley good-humoredly.

"Why, it just seems to me that if the letters were arranged in alphabetical order it would be a great deal easier to get them when one was in a hurry."

"It would seem so on the face of it," agreed Mr. Hawley, pleased by the lad's intelligence. "Printers, however, never arrange type that way. Instead, they put in the spot nearest at hand the letters they will use oftenest. It saves time. The men soon become accustomed to the position of these and can put their hands on them quickly and without the least trouble. The largest compartments in the drawers are given over to the letters most commonly in use, such as vowels and frequently recurring consonants. The letter Z you will notice has only a small space allowed it; X, too, is not much in demand."

"I see."

"Take one of these letters out and examine it."

Paul did so.

It was a thin bar of what appeared to be lead and was an inch long. On the end of it a single letter was cast.

"Besides these cases of letters, we have drawers of marks and signs arranged according to the same system, those most often in use being at the front of the drawer."

"It must have taken forever to hunt up the right letters and spell out the words before linotypes were invented," mused Paul.

"Yes, any amount of time was wasted that way," said Mr. Hawley. "The strain on the eyes was, too, something appalling. It is quite another matter to sit at a keyboard and with the pressure of a key assemble the proper matrices, as the type molds are called, and arrange in desired order correctly spaced and punctuated lines of type. Come over here and see how the work is done."

Crossing the floor, they stood before a machine where an operator was busy fingering a keyboard as if it were a typewriter. As he touched each key, it released a letter, and at the back of the machine Paul could see the silvery gleam as the miniature bar of metal dropped down and slipped into its place in the lengthening series of words. As soon as the row increased to line length, it moved along and a new line of words was assembled. The process was fascinating and the boy watched it spellbound.

"That's corking!" he at last burst out.

"It is a marvelous invention, certainly," responded Mr. Hawley, delighted by the enthusiasm of the *March Hare's* editor.

"What metal is used for casting type?" inquired Paul suddenly. "It looks like lead."

"It is not pure lead," Mr. Hawley answered. "That metal has been found to be much too soft; it soon wears down and loses its outline and its sharp edges. So an alloy of antimony is mixed with the lead and a composition is made that is harder and more durable."

"It must be quite a stunt to get the mixture just right," remarked Paul.

Again the newspaper man smiled with pleasure. It was a satisfaction to have so intelligent an audience.

"You have put your finger on a very important feature of the newspaper business," he rejoined. "The man who prepares the metal solution and keeps it at just the proper degree of temperature for casting is the person to whom the printer owes no small measure of his success. When we go downstairs, we shall see how the forms that are set here are cast in two large metal sections that fit on the two halves of the cylindrical rollers of the press. A mold of the form is first made from a peculiar kind of cardboard, a sort of *papier-mâché*, and by forcing hot metal into this mold a cast, or stereotype, of the page is taken. It is from this metal stereotype that the paper is printed. After the two sections are fastened securely upon the cylinders and inked by machinery, the great webs of paper at either end of the press unroll, and as they move over the rapidly turning wheels, your daily newspaper is printed for you."

"Are we going to see it done?" asked Paul eagerly.

"We certainly are," said Mr. Hawley, leading the way toward the elevator.

"Of course the compositors have to be very sure before the forms go to the stereotype casting room that there are no mistakes in them, I suppose," Paul ventured thoughtfully.

"Yes. There is no correcting the stereotype after it is once made," replied Mr. Hawley. "Everything is corrected and any exchange of letters made before it is cast. Men who handle type constantly become very expert in detecting errors, many compositors being able to read type upside down, or in reversed order, as easily as you can read a straightforward line of printed matter."

Mr. Hawley paused.

"In addition to this department," he presently continued, "is the room where the plates for the color section of the paper are prepared. After the drawing for the pictures is made, it is outlined on a block of metal and afterward cut out, so that the design remains in relief; then the impression is taken with colored inks, a separate printing being made for each color in turn, except where the colors are permitted to fuse before they dry in order to produce a secondary tone. You doubtless have seen the lithograph process and know how the first printing colors all the parts of the picture that are red, for example; the next impression prints the blue parts; and the third those that are green."

"Yes, I've seen posters printed."

"Then you know how the work is done."

"And it is for printing this colored supplement that the color-decks at each end of the big press are used?"

"Precisely. We often run these colored sections of the Sunday edition off some weeks in advance, as they are independent parts of the paper and need not necessarily be turned out at the last moment as the news sections must."

"I see."

"We also have our designing rooms for the drawing of fashion pictures, and the illustrations to accompany advertisements. All that is a department in itself, and a most interesting branch of the work. These cuts are prepared on sheets of metal and are cast and printed as the rest of the paper is; they are set into the forms and stereotyped by the same method as the printed matter. When we want reproductions from photographs we have a photo-engraving department where by means of a very powerful electric light we can reproduce pictures of all sorts; pen-drawings, facsimiles of old prints, photographs, and every variety of picture imaginable. These are developed on a sheet of metal instead of on a glass plate and then reproduced."

"That is the way you get the fine picture sheets that you enjoy so much, Paul," put in Mr. Wright.

"The photo-engraving took the place of the woodcut," Mr.

Hawley explained. "The process has been constantly improved until now we are able to get wonderfully artistic results."

"I had no idea there were so many different departments required to get out a paper," remarked Paul slowly. "It is an awful piece of work, isn't it?"

Their guide laughed.

"It is quite a project," he answered. "Of course, much of it becomes routine, and we think nothing about it. But I am sure that few persons who read the papers realize the great amount of time and thought that goes into turning out a good, up-to-date, artistically illustrated newspaper. The mere mechanical toil required is enormous; and in addition to this labor there is all the bustle, rush, and rivalry attending the securing of the latest news. The editorial office has its set of problems, as you know, if you yourself get out a paper."

"I've been so absorbed in the machinery that I forgot the editorial end of it for a moment," Paul said.

"Don't forget it, for it is the backbone of the business," replied Mr. Hawley. "All that part of our work is conducted as systematically as the rest. Each editorial writer and reporter is detailed to his particular work and must have his copy in promptly; he must know his facts and write them up with accuracy, charm, and spirit, the articles must also have the punch that will carry them and make people interested in reading them. A writer who can't turn out this sort of stuff has no place in the newspaper world. Every article that comes in is either used, returned, or filed away and catalogued for future reference; we call the room where the envelopes containing such matter are stacked the graveyard. Every newspaper has its graveyard. Into it goes stuff that has perhaps been paid for and never printed; clippings that can be used for reference; every sort of material. We can put our hand on any article filed, at a moment's notice. Come in and see for yourself the great tiers of shelves with the contents of each shelf classified and marked."

Paul followed him.

There indeed was the room, its shelves reaching to its ceiling and as neatly and completely arranged as they would be in a library. Sections were given over to business interests; to well-known men and women; to accidents; to shipping; to material of every description.

The visitors could not, however, delay to investigate this department, fascinating as it was. They were hurried on to another floor and were shown where all the accounts of advertisers were computed by means of an automatic device that registered the space taken by a specific firm and the price of such space. There was also a circulation department where lists of subscribers and records of their subscriptions were filed and billed.

Such ingenious contrivances were new to the village boy and his eyes widened. "I think we ought to pay more for our papers," he gasped. "I had no idea that publishing a newspaper meant so much work. I don't think we pay half enough money for all this trouble."

Mr. Hawley smiled.

"Sometimes I don't think we do either," he said.

"This is such a tremendous plant!" the boy went on breathlessly.

"Our paper is more of an undertaking, then, than your *March Hare.*"

"Well, rather!" chuckled Paul. "I thought we had quite a proposition until I saw all this. Now the mere writing of copy seems like nothing at all. What a job it is to print the stuff after you get it!"

"They say there is no better way to become cheered up than to take a peep at some other fellow's tribulations," Mr. Hawley declared. "Now suppose you go down to the press room and see some of ours at first hand."

He led the way to an elevator that dropped them quickly to the basement of the building.

"Do they always put the presses downstairs?" asked Paul.

"Practically always, yes," replied Mr. Hawley. "It is necessary to do so because of the immense weight of the presses. The problems of the vibration of machinery and the support of its weight always govern all factory construction and the building of plants of a similar nature. Most newspaper presses are therefore placed on solid ground, or as near it as possible, in order to minimize the difficulties arising from these two conditions. Some years ago, however, the *Boston Post* ventured an innovation by arranging its presses one over the other, three in a tier; and as the experiment has proved a success, many other large newspapers in various parts of the country have followed their example."

"If floor space can be economized it must be a great saving to newspaper plants whose buildings are in the heart of a city; real estate is no small item of expense," observed Mr. Wright.

"Precisely," agreed Mr. Hawley. "Yet high as were rentals and taxes, no one had had the courage to try a press constructed on another plan. It meant, of course, a new set of difficulties to solve. I happen to know, for instance, that when the floor for the sub-basement of the *Post* was constructed, the beams were set close enough together to support a weight of four hundred pounds to each square foot of space. This was not entirely necessary but it was done as a precaution against accident. Sometimes the mammoth rolls of paper fed into the presses fall when being hoisted into place and drop with a crash. If the floor were not strong the whole fifteen hundred pounds might go through and carry everything with it. The builders wished to be prepared for an emergency of this sort."

"They were wise."

"They could take no chances," said Mr. Hawley gravely. "The cellars, you see, run five stories below ground. They had to dig down, down, down to get the room they needed. The disadvantage of this is that all materials and all the printed papers as well have to be hoisted to and from the ground floor, and air and water must be pumped from the street level. Nevertheless, that this can be done has been proved. The questions of heating and ventilation are the most serious ones, for in the press rooms the thermometer cannot be permitted to vary more than a few degrees, either in winter or summer; any marked difference in temperature instantly affects the flow of the ink, causing no end of trouble. For that reason we have fans and all sorts of mechanical contrivances to keep the rooms at the desired heat."

"I should think you had conquered almost every imaginable difficulty," Mr. Wright remarked.

"Pretty nearly," returned Mr. Hawley good-naturedly.

They had now reached the lowest floor and the press rooms were a whir of noise and clatter. As the three entered, the hum of the machinery rendered further speech impossible.

Paul gazed up at the presses that towered high above his head.

There was the mighty machine and there were the hurrying workers, walking about it; some stood on the cement floor, and others moved here and there along the small swinging platforms that circled the upper part of the leviathan. In mid-air, held by mighty chains, hung the rolls of blank paper that were soon to be transformed into newspapers. As the vast spools of unprinted material were reeled off, the ribbons of whiteness passed like a spider's web in and out the turning wheels, and as they moved over the inked cylinders that printed them on both sides, the happenings of the world were recorded with lightning speed. In the meantime into the racks below were constantly dropping papers neatly folded,—papers that were finished and had each section arranged in its proper place; and to Paul's amazement an automatic machine counted these as they came from the press.

Whenever a certain number of papers were counted out a man came forward, hoisted the lot to his shoulder and disappeared into the elevator with it; or handed it to some one whose it duty it was to load it on to a truck, carry it upstairs, and put it into one of the myriad wagons that waited at the curb for its load. As fast as these wagons were filled they dashed off, bearing the Sunday editions to railway stations for shipping, or to distributing centers throughout the city; others had wrappers put on them and were dispatched to the mailing department to be addressed and forwarded to patrons who lived out of town.

"Some business, eh, Paul?" said Mr. Wright.

"You bet it is!"

"About one third of all the wood-pulp paper produced in America goes into newspapers and periodicals," Mr. Hawley managed to shout above the uproar of the whirling wheels. "That is where so many of our spruce, poplar, and hemlock trees go. Telephone books, telephone blanks, transfers for electric cars, city directories, play bills, consume a lot of paper; then in addition to the papers printed in English there are in America papers printed in fifty different foreign languages."

"I don't wonder there was a shortage of paper during the war," stammered Paul.

"It hit us pretty close," Mr. Hawley owned. "Our Sunday editions had to be curtailed a good deal, and many of the monthly publications were put out of business entirely by the high cost of paper. The monthly magazine is, you know, a great seller in rural communities. A newspaper is usually a local affair; but the monthly circulates all over the country and is not by any means confined to the district in which it is published."

"It makes a nice lot of work for the Post Office Department," put in Mr. Wright jestingly.

"Yes, it does," agreed Mr. Hawley.

"I suppose book publishing and music publishing take more paper," mused Paul.

"Yes. The printing of music is an expensive and fussy piece of work, too. It must be accurately done, and done by men who are experienced in that special kind of work. One misprint will cause a discord and throw the music out of sale. Of course if a song turns out to be popular, a small fortune is often reaped from it; but if it is not, the cost of getting it out is so great that little is netted by the publishers."

They moved on into another room where it was more quiet, leaving the hum of the presses behind them.

"This," explained Mr. Hawley, "is the stereotype-casting room of which I told you. It is here that the *papier-mâché* forms made from the forms you saw in linotype are brought and cast in solid pieces for the presses. Let us watch the process. You can see how they fasten the paper impression around this mold so that the cast of it can be taken. The hot metal is run in, and pressed into every depression of the cardboard. The thickness of these semi-cylindrical casts is carefully specified and over there is a machine that pares off or smooths away all superfluous material so that they come out exactly the proper thickness; otherwise they would not fit the rollers of the press."

Paul watched. Sure enough! After being cast, the sections of stereotype were put into the machine indicated and moved quickly along, being planed off as they went; when they emerged the wrong side of them was smooth and even.

"This kettle or tank of hot metal," went on Mr. Hawley, pointing to a vat of seething composition, "has to be kept, as I explained to you, at a specified degree of heat if we are to get successful stereotypes of our forms. Therefore a great deal depends on the skill and judgment of the man who prepares and melts down the mixture bubbling in that kettle. Without his brain and experience there could be no newspapers."

As he spoke Mr. Hawley waved a salutation to the workman in blue overalls who was studying the indicator beside the furnace.

"That indicator tells the exact temperature of the melted solution in the kettle; also the temperature of the furnace. There can be no variation in heat without hindering the work of casting, and perhaps wrecking the casts and wasting a quantity of material. So on that little chap over there by the fire hangs our fate."

The workman heard the words and smiled, and Paul smiled in return.

"Do they make stereotypes for circular rollers and print books this same way?" he asked.

"No. Most books are electrotyped, the machinery being much less complex than is the newspaper press. A rotary press cannot do such fine or accurate work."

For a moment they lingered, watching the busy scene with its shifting figures. Then they stepped into the elevator and were shot up to the street level. The hands of the clock stood at eleven when at last they emerged upon the sidewalk.

Paul sighed.

"Tired?"

"Rather, sir; aren't you?"

"Well, I just feel as if I had played sixteen holes of golf," Mr. Wright replied. They laughed together.

"But, Jove! It was worth it though, wasn't it?" cried Paul.

"I think so."

"I, too! Only," added the boy, "I still believe we ought to pay more for our newspapers."

CHAPTER XV

THE DECISION

For the next few days after his return from Boston Paul thought and talked of little else save the great newspaper press that he had seen. Beside a project as tremendous as the publication of a widely circulated daily the *March Hare* became a pitifully insignificant affair.

Nevertheless the *March Hare* was not to be thrust aside. It clamored for attention. Its copy came in as before from students and staff, and mixed with this material were some exceptionally fine articles from parents and distant alumnæ. Judge Damon had taken to contributing a short, crisp editorial almost every month, something of civic or national importance; and two of Burmingham's graduates who were in France sent letters that added an international flavor to the magazine. Never had the issues been so good. Certainly the monthly so modestly begun had ripened into an asset that all the town would regret to part with.

In the meantime graduation was approaching and the day was drawing near when 1920 must bid good-by to the familiar halls of the school, and instead of standing and looking down from the top of the ladder, as it now did, it must set forth into the turmoil of real life where its members would once again be beginners. What an ironic transformation that would be!

A senior was a person looked up to by the entire student body, a dignitary to be treated with profound respect. But once outside the sheltering walls of his Alma Mater he would suddenly become a very ordinary being who, like Samson shorn of his locks, would enter business or college a weak, timid neophyte. It seemed absurd that such a change could be wrought in so short a time.

But before the day when the diplomas with their stiff white bows would be awarded, the future fate of the *March Hare* must be decided. Every recurrence of this thought clouded Paul's brow. He still had intact Mr. Carter's fifty-dollar bill. It was as crisp and fresh as on the day the magnate of Burmingham had put it into his hand, and the typewriter Paul coveted still glistened in the window of a shop on the main street. Day after day he had vacillated between the school and that fascinating store window, and each day he had looked, envied, and come home again. It was now so late that the purchase of this magic toy would be of little use to him. Nevertheless, he wanted it. Every night when he went to bed he quieted his conscience's accusations of cowardice by arguing that the money had not been spent. But not spending it, he was forced to own, was far from being the same thing as returning it. It was strange that it should be so hard for him to part with that money!

In the interim he had cashed in his war stamps and with the additional sum he had earned for doing the chores around the place he and Melville Carter had paid the bill the *March Hare* owed and deposited the remainder of their combined cash in the bank, so that the accounts now stood even. Whatever should now become of the magazine, its slate was a clean one so far as its financial standing went.

Having thus disposed of all debts and entanglements, only

the adjustment of the deal with Mr. Carter remained. This was not so easily to be cleared from Paul's path.

It was his first thought in the morning, his last at night. He could never escape from it. Whenever he was in jubilant mood and in a flood of boyish happiness had forgotten it, it arose like a specter to torment him. What was he going to do with that money that he had kept so long? And what was he going to say to his classmates to earn it,—for earn it he must, since he had accepted it. It was a wretched position to be in. Why hadn't he given the bill back to the great man that day in the office? Or if he had no opportunity then, why hadn't he carried it promptly to the *Echo* building the next morning? He might have gone to Mr. Carter's house with it. There were a score of ways it might have been delivered to its rightful owner. Alas, he had been very weak, and by drifting along and taking no positive action had got himself into the dilemma in which he now floundered.

It was the president of 1921 who suddenly brought him up with a sharp turn by remarking one day:

"Well, Kip, you people of 1920 have certainly set us a pretty pace on the *March Hare*. I don't know whether, when it descends to us, we shall be able to keep it up to your standard or not."

"Descends to you!" repeated Paul vaguely.

"Yes. Of course 1920 is going to pass it on. You fellows can't very well take it with you," laughed the junior.

Paul evaded a direct answer.

"You never can tell which way a hare will run," he replied.

"You can usually figure on the direction he will take, though," retorted the under-classman, whose name was Converse. "1920 has done the school a big service by founding the paper and outlining its policy. My father was saying only last night that the magazine was well worth putting on a permanent business basis. He said that if an experienced publishing house had the handling of it it could be made into a money-making proposition—that is if everybody, young and old, would keep up their same enthusiasm for turning in stuff so the tone of the thing was not spoiled."

"I believe that, too."

"It wouldn't be such a bad idea if next year we could get in an experienced hand to help us, would it?"

The moment Paul dreaded had come.

He summoned all his dignity.

"I am not sure," he answered, "just what 1920 will decide to do with the paper when we finish the year. We may sell it."

"What! You don't mean sell it to an outsider?"

"We have an opportunity to do so."

"But—but—how could you? It's the property of the school, isn't it?" stammered Converse.

"No, not as I see it. A few of us 1920 fellows started it and have done all the work, or the bulk of it. If we choose to sell it, I don't see why we haven't a right to."

"But—Great hat, Kip! You certainly wouldn't do that!" protested the junior.

"Why not?"

"Because—well—it would be so darn yellow," burst out the other boy. "Even if the thing is yours—why—," he broke off helplessly. "And anyway, how could you? Any number of people are interested in it."

"They could keep on being interested in it."

"You mean somebody else would publish it?"

"Yes."

"As it is now?"

"Practically. They would give it a more professional touch, no doubt."

"Do you think for a second that in the hands of a cut and dried publisher it would be the same?" asked Converse hotly. "Do you imagine people would send in articles to it as they do now?"

"I don't see why not."

"They wouldn't—not on your life! Why, the reason that everybody has pitched in and written for us was precisely because the thing was not professional, and they knew they would be free of criticism. The columns have become a sort of town forum, my father said. Do you think you could get the same people to speak out under different conditions? Judge Damon, for instance, has repeatedly refused to write for the professional press. He could get a fat sum for such editorials as he writes for us if he wanted to sell them. Father said so. Besides, what's to become of 1921 if you sell out the *March Hare*? We couldn't run a rival paper. If the *Hare* continued, of course people would take a thing that was already established and that they knew about, especially as it had been so bully. It would end us so far as a school magazine was concerned."

Paul offered no reply.

"I'd call it a darn mean trick if you put such a deal over," persisted Converse indignantly, "and I guess everybody else would. I suppose you would have the legal right to sell out if you wanted to; but it has been tacitly understood from the first that the paper was started for the good of the school and would be handed down to your successors."

"I don't see why everybody should jump at that conclusion."

"Because it is the natural, square thing to do. Anybody would tell you so."

"I don't need to take a popular vote to settle my affairs," returned Paul haughtily.

"You may have to in this case," called Converse, turning on his heel.

The incident left Paul nettled and disturbed, and in consequence the Latin recitation that followed went badly; so did his chemistry exam.

The instant recess came he signalled to his closest literary associates and beckoning them into an empty classroom, banged the door.

"See here, you chaps," he began, "I've something to put up to you. We have had an offer to sell the *March Hare*. How does the proposition strike you?"

The boys regarded their leader blankly.

"You mean to—to—sell it out for money?" inquired one of the group stupidly.

Paul laughed.

"What else could we sell it out for, fat-head?" he returned good-humoredly.

"But—to sell it out for cash, as it stands—you mean that?"

"Righto!"

"Somebody wants to buy it?"

"Yes."

"Gee!"

"We certainly are some little editors," chuckled Melville Carter. "Who is the bidder, Kip?"

"Yes, Kip, who wants it?" came breathlessly from one and another of the group.

It was evident they had no inkling who the prospective purchaser was.

"Mr. Carter."

"Carter—of the *Echo?*"

"My father?" gasped Melville, dumfounded.

"Yes, he has offered to buy us out," continued Paul steadily. "He'll give us a certain sum of money to divide between us."

"But could we sell?" asked Melville slowly.

"The thing is ours, isn't it?" replied Paul. "Haven't we planned it, built it up, and done all the work?"

"Yes," Melville admitted in a half-convinced tone.

"I suppose, in point of fact, it really is ours," remarked Donald Hall. "But it would be a rotten, low-down trick for us to sell it away from the school and from 1921, I think."

"Did my father suggest it?" queried Melville.

"Yes. He is quite keen on it. He says it can be made a paying proposition."

There was a pause.

"What do you think of the offer, Kip?"

It was one of the members of the editorial staff who spoke.

"I?"

Paul turned crimson.

The question was painfully direct.

"Yes," demanded the other boys. "What do you say, Kipper? What's your opinion?"

Paul looked uneasily into the faces of his friends. Their eyes were fixed eagerly upon him. In their gaze he could read confidence and respect. A flood of scorn for his own cowardice overwhelmed him. He straightened himself.

"If you want to know what I honestly think," he heard himself saying, "I'd call it a beastly shame to sell out."

There was a shout of approval. There was only one boy who did not join in the hubbub; it was Weldon.

"How much would Carter give us apiece?" he asked.

"Shut up, you old grafter!" snapped Roger Bell. "There's

no use in your knowing. You're voted down already. Kip's perfectly right. We don't want the *Echo's* money."

"Tell Carter there's nothing doing," put in a high voice.

"You decide, then, to bequeath the *March Hare* to 1921 with our blessing?" asked Paul, with a laugh.

"Sure we do!"

"We are poor but honest!" piped Charlie Decker, rolling his eyes up to the ceiling with a gesture that brought a roar of applause. Charlie was the class joke.

A gong sounded.

"There's the bell!" cried somebody. "All aboard for Greek A!"

Melville Carter reached across and rumpled up Donald Hall's hair.

"Quit it, kiddo!" protested Donald nervously, drawing back from his chum's grasp.

"What's the matter with you, all of a sudden?" demanded Melville, surprised.

"Nothing! Cut it out, that's all."

"Aren't you coming to Greek?" asked young Carter.

"In a minute. Trot along; I want to speak to Kip."

The throng filed out until only Donald and Paul were in the room.

The editor-in-chief was standing alone at the window. For the first time in weeks he was drawing the breath of freedom. A weight seemed removed from his soul. He had been weak and vacillating, but when the test had come he had not been false either to himself or to his friends. That at least was something.

Thinking that he was alone, he drew from his pocket the fifty-dollar bill that was to have been the price of his undoing, and looked at it. He would take it back that very day to Mr. Carter and confess that he had not fulfilled the contract the newspaper owner had tried to force upon him. A smile parted his lips. It was as he turned to leave the room that he encountered Donald Hall.

The expression of the lad's face gave him a start; there was shame, regret, suffering in it.

"What's the matter, Don?" Paul asked.

The boy tried to speak but no words came.

"You're not sick, old chap?"

"No. Why?"

"You look so darn queer. Anything I can do for you?"

"N—o. No, I guess not. I just waited to see if you were coming along."

"Yes, I'm coming right now," returned Paul briskly. "We'll both have to be hopping, or we'll be late. So long! See you later."

The boys passed out into the corridor together and there fled in opposite directions.

But Donald's face haunted Paul through the rest of the morning. What could be the matter with the boy?

CHAPTER XVI

AN AMAZING MIRACLE

At the close of the session that day Paul walked with reluctant feet toward the office of the *Echo*.

It was with the greatest difficulty that he had shaken off the fellows one by one,—Melville, Roger Bell, Donald Hall, Billie Ransom, and the other boys; he had even evaded Converse who, having heard the good news, came jubilantly toward him with the words:

"1920 is all right! She never was yellow, and I knew she wouldn't change color at this late date."

Paul smiled and passed on. Yes, he had done the square thing; he knew it perfectly well. Nor did he regret his action. On the contrary he was more light-hearted than he had been for a long time. Nevertheless he did not exactly fancy the coming interview with Mr. Carter.

He had called up the *Echo*, and by a bit of good fortune had managed not only to get into touch with the editorial office but to reach the publisher himself. If the business at hand were important, Mr. Carter would see him. It was important, Paul said. Then he might come promptly at four o'clock and the magnate would give him half an hour.

It was almost four now. The hands of the clock were moving toward the dreaded moment only too fast.

Soon, the boy reflected with a little shiver up his spine, he would be in the bare little sanctum of the great man, facing those piercing eyes and handing back the fifty-dollar bill that had lain in his pocket for so many weeks; and he would be confessing that he had failed in his mission,—nay, worse than that, that he had not even tried to accomplish it. It would, of course, be impossible to explain how, when the crisis had come, something within him had leaped into being,—something that had automatically prevented him from doing what was wrong and forced him to do what was right. He took small credit to himself for his deed. It was his good genius that deserved the praise. He wondered idly as he went along whether this potent force had been his conscience or his soul. Well, it did not matter much; the result was the same. Conscience, soul, whatever it was, it was sending him back to Carter with that unspent bribe money.

He was glad of it. Had he but done this weeks before, he would have been spared days and weeks of uncertainty and worry. He realized now that he had never felt right, felt happy about that bill. Yet although his bonds were now to be broken, and he was to be free at last, the shattering of his fetters was not to be a pleasant process. He knew Mr. Carter too well to deceive himself into imagining that the affair would pass off lightly. Mr. Carter was a proud man. He would not like having his gift hurled back into his face. Nor would he enjoy being beaten. Greater than any value he would set on the ownership of the *March Hare* would loom the consciousness that he had been defeated, balked by a lot of schoolboys, by one boy in particular. The incident would ruffle his vanity and annoy him mightily.

It was with this knowledge that Paul stepped into the elevator. How he wished there was some escape from the approaching interview! If only Mr. Carter should prove to be busy, or be out!

But Mr. Carter was not busy, and he was not out! On the contrary, the clerk told Paul that the great man was expecting him and had given orders that he was to come into the office as soon as he arrived.

Gulping down a nervous tremor, the lad steadied himself and put his hand on the knob of the awful ground-glass door. Once on the other side of it and all retreat would be cut off. Not that he really wished to retreat. It was only that he dreaded.... The knob turned and he was inside the room.

Mr. Carter was at his desk dictating a letter; he finished the last sentence and motioned his stenographer to withdraw. He then asked Paul to sit down in the chair the girl had vacated.

"Well, you've got some news for me," he began without preamble.

"Yes, sir," Paul replied. "We had a class meeting to-day. I couldn't put your deal through, Mr. Carter. I'm bringing back the money."

He laid the bill on the publisher's desk.

Mr. Carter paid no heed to the money. Instead he kept his eyes on the boy before him, studying him through the smoke that clouded the room.

"You couldn't pull it off, eh?" he said sharply. "I'm sorry to hear that. What was the trouble?"

"I didn't try to pull it off."

"Didn't try!"

"No, sir."

"You mean you didn't advise your staff to sell out?"

"I spoke against it."

"Against it!" snarled Carter, leaning forward in his chair.

The room was breathlessly still.

"You see," explained the boy, "the more I thought about it

the less I approved of what you wanted me to do. I tried to think it was straight but I didn't really think so. When the fellows asked my honest opinion, I simply had to tell them the truth."

Mr. Carter made no comment, nor did his eyes leave Paul's face, but he drew his shaggy brows together and scowled.

"So," went on Paul desperately, "I've brought your money back to you. It's the same bill you gave me. I didn't spend it. Somehow I couldn't bring myself to."

There was an awkward pause. Paul got to his feet.

"I'm—I'm—sorry to have disappointed you, Mr. Carter," he murmured in a low tone as he moved across the room to go. "You have been mighty kind to us boys."

The door was open and he was crossing the threshold before the man at the desk spoke; then he called:

"Hold on a minute, son."

Paul turned.

"Shut that door."

Wondering, the boy obeyed.

Mr. Carter took up the greenback lying before him.

"So you've been carrying that money round with you ever since I gave it to you, have you?"

"Yes, sir."

"It's a long time; some weeks."

"Yes," stammered Paul. "I ought to have brought it back to you before."

"I could charge you interest on it."

The smile that accompanied the speech escaped Paul.

"I'll pay whatever you think proper," he said.

"Nonsense, boy! I was only joking," the publisher hastened to say. "But tell me something; what was it you wanted that money for? You must have needed it badly or you would not have been threatening to sell out your Liberty Bond."

"I was going to buy a typewriter, sir."

"Oh! And you didn't get it. That was a pity."

The man tapped the edge of the bill he held against the desk thoughtfully. Paul waited for him to speak; but when after an interval he still remained silent the lad shifted uneasily from one foot to the other and remarked:

"I guess I'll be going along, sir. The half hour you were to give me is up."

Then Mr. Carter spoke.

"Will you shake hands with me, my boy, before you go, or have you too poor an opinion of me for that?"

"Indeed I haven't a poor opinion of you, Mr. Carter," replied Paul, with hearty sincerity. "You have always been mighty good to me. It's true I didn't like your *March Hare* proposition but—"

"Your father hasn't much use for me either, I'm afraid," Mr. Carter observed moodily.

"Dad thinks you bought up the election."

"He's right. I set out to win a majority in this town and I did it. But in order to beat a man as white as your father I had to resort to a pretty poor weapon. Everything was with him. Measured up side by side we weren't in the same class. He was by far the better man and I knew it. I couldn't beat him as to character but I could do it with money, and I did. It was a contemptible game. I've always despised myself for playing it. I wish you'd tell your dad so."

Paul could scarcely credit his ears.

"And about this school business," went on Mr. Carter—"you were just right, son. The school should continue the paper along the lines on which you have started it. It ought to remain the property of the students, too. All is, if next year they care to have the *Echo* print it, we'll donate the labor free. The school can pay the actual cost of materials and I'll see to the rest of it. I can afford to do one decent thing for Burmingham, I guess."

"Oh, Mr. Carter," gasped Paul, "that would be—"

But the man interrupted him.

"And there's a second-hand typewriter lying round here somewhere that you can have if you like. We are getting a new one of another make. You won't find this much worn I reckon, and I guess you can manage to get some work out of it. I'll send it round to your house to-morrow in my car."

"Why, sir, I can't—"

The great man put out his hand kindly.

"There, there, run along! I'm busy," he said. "Don't forget my message to your father."

"No, sir."

Then he added hurriedly:

"I don't know how to thank you, Mr. Carter."

"That's all right," nodded the publisher, cutting him short. "I've always had the greatest respect for your father. Tell him from me that he needn't be ashamed of his son."

With these parting words he waved Paul out of the office and the door closed.

CHAPTER XVII

THE CLOUDS CLEAR

When, glowing with happiness, Paul turned into his gate late in the afternoon, he was surprised to find Donald Hall impatiently pacing the driveway before the house. The boy's bicycle was against the fence and it was evident that he had been waiting some time, for a bunch of lilacs tied to the handle-bar hung limp and faded in the sun.

"How are you, old man," Paul called jubilantly. "What are you doing here?"

"Hanging around until you should heave into sight. I must say you take your time. Your mother has been expecting you every minute since school closed."

"I had to go to the *Echo* office and so got delayed."

"Did you tell Carter about the meeting?"

"Yes."

"How did he take it?"

"He was great—corking!"

"Really? I thought he'd cut up pretty rough."

"So did I; but he didn't. He's more decent than I gave him credit for being. I like Carter. He's all right."

"You're the first person I ever heard say so."

"Perhaps people don't know him," replied Paul warmly. "You can't judge a man hot off the bat. You've got to try him out."

Donald broke into a laugh.

"Oh, he's been tried out all right. People know him too well; that's the trouble."

Paul stiffened.

"Well, all I can say is that I've found Carter mighty kind. He's treated me white. If you knew as much about him as I do you'd say so too. In the meantime I'd thank you to remember he's my friend and not run him down."

There was an awkward pause. Donald dug the toe of his shoe into the gravel walk and fidgeted uneasily.

Paul waited a moment, then, attributing his chum's silence to resentment, he added in a gentler tone: "I didn't mean to pitch into you so hard, old chap; it's only that Carter has been so mighty generous that I couldn't bear to have you light into him that way."

Donald, however, despite the conciliatory tone, did not raise his head. Instead he continued to bore holes in the walk, automatically hollowing them out and filling them up again with the tip of his boot.

Paul endured the suspense until at last he could not endure it any longer.

"I say, Don, what's fussing you?" he burst out.

The visitor crimsoned.

"What makes you think anything is?" he asked, hedging.

"Well, you wouldn't be loafing around here, digging up our whole driveway, unless there was," persisted Paul good-humoredly. "Come, out with it! You're the darndest kid for getting into messes. What's happened to you now?"

There was an affectionate ring in the bantering words.

Donald smiled feebly. It was true that he was usually in some scrape or other. It was not that he did mean or vicious things; Donald Hall was far too fine a lad for that. But he never could resist playing a prank, and whenever he played one he was invariably caught. Even though every other member of the crowd got away, Donald never contrived to. The boys declared this was because he was slow and clumsy. But the truth really was that he was wont, in unselfish fashion, to let every one else go first and was in consequence the unlucky victim whom the pursuers were sure to capture. The fleeing culprits were generally in too great haste to appreciate his altruism and he never enlightened them. He took his punishment, loyally refusing to peach on his chums. That was one reason Donald was such a favorite with his classmates. There was not a fellow in the school who had more friends. To be sure they called him "slow coach", "old tortoise", "fatty", and bestowed upon him many another gibing epithet, frankly telling him to his face that he was a big idiot. Nevertheless they did not conceal from him that he was the sort of idiot they all loved.

Hence it followed that when Paul saw his chum in the present disturbed frame of mind he was much distressed and immediately leaped to the conclusion that for the hundredth—nay, the five hundredth—time Don had been caught in the snares of justice.

"Come, come, Tortoise," he repeated; "tell a chap what's up with you."

"Kip," burst out Donald with sudden vehemence, "I've done a mighty mean thing."

"You!"

"Yes, sir."

"Bosh! You never did a mean thing in your life, kid."

"But I have now," smiled the lad wanly. "They say there always has to be a first time. I didn't start out to do it, though. Still, that doesn't help matters much, for it's ended that way."

"Going to let me in on it?" asked Paul, hoping to make the confession easier.

"Yes, I came over on purpose to tell you, Kip. It's the queerest mix-up you ever heard of. It's worried me no end. Sometimes, it's seemed as if I was going nutty."

"Fire ahead! Tell a man, can't you?"

"Well, you see a while ago my father sent me to deposit some money in the bank for him—a hundred-dollar bill. I put the envelope in my pocket, carefully as could be. I remember perfectly doing it. I didn't go anywhere but straight down town, either. Well, anyhow, when I got to the bank the money was gone! It wasn't in my pocket; it wasn't anywhere about me."

He stopped an instant.

"You can imagine how I felt. My father had cautioned me not to lose that money on my life. I hadn't the nerve to tell him. Somehow I thought that if I could just smooth the matter over for a little while the envelope with the money in it would turn up. I was certain I couldn't have lost it."

Again he paused.

"At first I thought I'll sell a Liberty bond I had and put my hundred in the bank to dad's credit. Then I happened to think that my father had the bond locked up in his safe-deposit box and that I couldn't get at it without telling him. I didn't know what to do. I simply hadn't the courage to go home and tell the truth. You wouldn't like to face your father and tell him you'd lost a cool hundred of his cash for him. Besides, I was sure it wasn't lost. I felt morally certain I had somehow misplaced that envelope and that it would come to light. I hunted all day, though, through my pockets and everywhere I could think of and it didn't appear. I began to get scared. What was I going to do? When the bank statement came in my father would see right off that the money had not been deposited. And anyway, even if he didn't, it was only square to tell him what I'd done. I was casting round for a way out when that noon Mel called me and asked me if I'd do an errand for him on the way home. He wanted me to stop at the bank as I passed and put in some *March Hare* money. It was a hundred dollars and it seemed to drop right out of the sky into my hands. I decided to deposit it to my father's credit and trust to finding the sum I'd lost to square up the school accounts."

A light of understanding began to break in on Paul.

He waited.

"I guess you know what's coming," Donald murmured.

"No, I don't."

"Well, somebody does," declared the boy wretchedly. "That's what's got me fussed. I chance to know how the *March Hare* books stood. Somebody's made good that money I took—made it good without saying a word about it."

Donald, studying his friend's face, saw a gleam of satisfaction pass over it.

"Kip!" he whispered, "was it you? Did you put the money back when you found it gone from the treasury?"

"Mel and I divided it. We found the accounts short and of course we had to do something. We thought we'd made a mistake in the books," explained Paul. "So we turned in the sum and evened things up."

"Without telling anybody?"

"Yes; what was the use of blabbing it all over town?"

"Gee!"

Donald fumbled in his pocket.

"Well, I've found the hundred, Kip. Here it is safe and sound. The envelope had slipped down through a hole in the lining of my pocket. The other day when I was hunting for my fountain pen, I discovered the rip. You bet I was glad. I'd have made that money good somehow. I wasn't going to take it. I hope you'll believe I'm not such a cad as that. But what I ought to have done was to tell my father in the first place. It's been an awful lesson to me. I've worried myself thin—I have, Kip. You needn't laugh."

Nevertheless, Paul did laugh. He couldn't help it when he looked at Donald's conscience-smitten expression. Moreover he could now afford to laugh.

But Donald was not so easily consoled.

"I'm almighty sorry, Kip," he said. "The whole thing has been rotten. Think of you and Mel Carter turning in your cash to make the bank accounts square. Where on earth did you each get your fifty?"

"Some of it was money I'd earned and put aside toward a typewriter; and the rest I got by cashing in my war stamps."

"Oh, I say!"

Regret and mortification overwhelmed the culprit.

"It's no matter now, Don."

"But it is, old chap. I suppose that knocked you out of buying your typewriter. It's a darn shame."

"I was pretty sore, Don—no mistake!" admitted Paul. "But it's all right now. The accounts are O.K.; I shall get my money back; and I have a typewriter into the bargain. Mr. Carter has just given me a second-hand machine they weren't using."

"Did he know about this muddle?"

"Not a yip! He did know, though, that I wanted the typewriter."

"Well, I'll take back all I ever said about him," cried Donald. "He's a trump! As for you, Kip—you deserve a hundred type-writers! It's all-fired good of you not to rub this in. I know I've caused you a lot of trouble and I'm sorry. That's all I can say."

"Shut up, Tortoise. It's all right now," repeated Paul. "Only don't go appropriating any more funds that don't belong to you. We might jail you next time. Taking other people's cash isn't much of a stunt."

"You bet it isn't!" cried Donald heartily. "When you do it you think it's going to be easy as fiddle to slip it back again; but it doesn't seem to turn out that way. Jove, but I'm glad I'm clear of this mess!"

"I guess we both will sleep better to-night than we have for one while," called Paul, moving toward the house. "So long, Don!"

"So long, Kipper. And don't you go losing that money. It's caused too much worry already."

"I'll take care of it—don't you fuss about that. There are no rips in my coat lining."

Thus they parted—the happiest pair of boys in all Burmingham.

CHAPTER XVIII

GRADUATION

Thus did Paul's troubles dissolve in air and with the June winds blow far away. In the meantime graduation came and the essay he delivered was clicked off on Mr. Carter's typewriter which, considering the fact that it was a second-hand one, was an amazingly fresh and unscarred machine.

Nor was this all. After the graduation exercises had come to a close, and the audience was passing out of the building, Mr. Cameron and the publisher of the *Echo* came face to face in the corridor. They had not met since the famous mayoral campaign when Carter, by means of wholesale bribery, had swept all before him. Hence the present encounter was an awkward one and many a citizen of Burmingham stopped to witness the drama. Had the two men been able to avoid the clash they would undoubtedly have done so; but the hallway was narrow and escape was impossible. Here they were wedged in the crowd, each of them having come hither to see his son take his diploma. It was a day of rejoicing and no time for grudges.

Melville was at his father's elbow while at Mr. Cameron's heels tagged Paul, hot, tired, but victorious.

The instant the group collided the magnate's hand shot out and gripped that of the editor-in-chief of the *March Hare*.

"Well, youngster, I'm proud of you!" he exclaimed. "You did well. We shall be making a newspaper man of you yet."

Then, glancing up into the face of the lad's father, he added with hesitating graciousness:

"I—I—congratulate you on your son, Cameron."

Mr. Cameron was not to be outdone.

"And I on yours, Mr. Carter. Melville is a fine boy. You must be glad that he has done so well."

"Oh, Melville's not perfect," declared Mr. Carter, obviously pleased, "but he is all the boy we've got and we like him."

There was a pause.

"Our young representatives have done pretty well on this paper of theirs, haven't they?" remarked Mr. Carter the next moment.

"They certainly have," agreed Mr. Cameron. "The *March Hare* is a very readable and creditable little magazine. You've done both the school and the community a service, Carter, by printing it."

"I've made some blunders in my life, Cameron, for which I have since been very sorry," the rich man said, looking significantly into Mr. Cameron's eyes. "But printing the *March Hare* was not one of them, thank God! We consider the school paper well worth printing," he added in a lighter tone. "Everything the *Echo* prints is worth while, you know."

Mr. Cameron laughed at the jest.

"I've been dragged into reading your august publication, you know," said he. "I subscribed to it against my will, I must own; however, I must confess that I have enjoyed it very much. If you'd change your party, Carter, and come into the proper political fold—"

Mr. Carter held up his hand.

"No propaganda, Cameron!" he declared good-naturedly. "We must learn wisdom of our children. Their paper is quite non-partisan. In fact," he continued, lapsing into seriousness, "the younger generation teaches us many things. I've learned a lesson or two from your son. You have put a great deal of your fineness of principle into him, Cameron. I hope you realize what a deep respect I entertain for you. I have always regretted the occurrences that parted us. If I had my life to live over again, my dear sir, there are some offenses that I should not repeat. An honor that one wins by foul means is an empty one. I took an unfair advantage of an honorable gentleman in the campaign of 1916 and I have always been sorry and longed to tell you so. I now offer you my hand. It is the only amendment I can make for the past."

The apology was a handsome one and Mr. Cameron was a big enough man to be forgiving.

Taking his enemy's palm in a warm grasp he said:

"We all blunder sometimes, Carter."

"An honest blunder is one thing; but pre-meditated mean-ness is quite another, Cameron. However, I appreciate your generosity. It is like you—on the same scale with the rest of your nature." Then to shift a subject that was embarrassing he remarked: "As for these young rascals of ours, I suppose a great career awaits each of them after college is over. Your son has a better brain than mine; but they are both promising fellows. I'd like to land Paul in an editorial position. He has a decided gift for such a job. Perhaps later on I may be able to help him, should he decide to take up such work permanently. I should be very proud to be of service either to you or him, Cameron."

"Thank you, sir," replied Mr. Cameron courteously.

Amid the pressing crowd they separated, the parents to go

home in a mood of satisfaction and happiness, and the boys to continue the day's festivities with a class banquet and a dance.

That banquet was a never-to-be-forgotten affair!

For weeks the class officers had been planning it and no detail was omitted that could add merriment and joy to the crowning event of 1920's career.

No sooner were the guests seated at the long table and the spread fairly begun than a stuffed rabbit, exquisitely decorated with the class colors, was borne into the room. This was, of course, the far-famed March Hare. Its advent was greeted with a storm of clapping.

Very solemnly it was elevated in Paul's hands and amid shouts and cheers was carried by the graduating editor-in-chief to the president of 1921 where, with an appropriate speech, it was surrendered into the keeping of the incoming seniors.

Then the banquet went on only to have its progress interrupted at intervals by bustling attendants who came rushing in with telegrams, special delivery letters, and telephone messages from the Hatter, the Red Queen, the Dormouse, and many another well-beloved Wonderland character. Afterward the Walrus and the Carpenter sang a song and then, with great acclaim and a crash of the orchestra, the folding doors opened and Alice herself, impersonating 1921, entered, gathered up the *March Hare,* and with a graceful little poem of farewell to 1920 took the head of the table.

With a sigh glad yet regretful, Paul surrendered his place.

He had longed for the day when he should be graduating from school and setting forth for college; but now that the moment had really arrived, he found himself not nearly so glad to depart from the High School as he had expected to be. Many a pleasant memory clustered about the four years he had spent in those familiar classrooms. And the comrades of those years,—he was parting from them, too. Some were scattering to the various colleges; some were going into business; others were to remain at home. Never again would they all travel the same path together. Alas, graduation had its tragic as well as its happy aspects!

Perhaps some such thought as this lurked deep down in the breast of every member of 1920, but for the sake of one another, and to make the last moments they were to spend together unclouded by sadness, each bravely struggled to banish this sinister reflection.

Hence the dance that followed the banquet was an uproarious affair. When one is young and all the world lies before, the conqueror Gloom is short-lived. So 1920 danced gayly until midnight, forgetful of every shadow, and when weary, sleepy, but triumphant, a half-jubilant, half-sorrowful lot of girls and boys betook themselves to their homes, it was with ringing cheers for the Burmingham High School, the class of 1920, the *March Hare*, Mr. Carter, its printer, and Paul Cameron, its editor-in-chief.